HERDSBOY

To Jane + Alan

Best Wishes

Paul

6-19-96

HERDSBOY

PAUL MEYER

Northwest Publishing, Inc.
Salt Lake City, Utah

Herdsboy

All rights reserved.
Copyright © 1993 Paul Meyer

Reproduction in any manner, in whole or in part,
in English or in other languages, or otherwise
without written permission of the publisher is prohibited.

This is a work of fiction.
All characters and events portrayed in this book are fictional,
and any resemblance to real people or incidents is purely coincidental.

For information address: Northwest Publishing, Inc.
6906 South 300 West, Salt Lake City, Utah 84047
JAC 9.29.94
Edited by: S. J. Davis

PRINTING HISTORY
First Printing 1995

ISBN: 1-56901-582-1

NPI books are published by Northwest Publishing, Incorporated,
6906 South 300 West, Salt Lake City, Utah 84047.
The name "NPI" and the "NPI" logo are trademarks belonging to
Northwest Publishing, Incorporated.

PRINTED IN THE UNITED STATES OF AMERICA.
10 9 8 7 6 5 4 3 2 1

1

The sky shimmered in the heat above the dry, brush-covered hillside. Halfway up the slope, Firingin stood, stork-like on one leg. He gazed at the spackle of white- and rust-colored cattle that foraged around him.

This day, as every day, he tended them while they grazed on the sun-scorched grasslands near the Lbaa clan's village. At twenty-seven beasts, the herd of his family was not the largest in the clan, but it contained only cattle, no goats or sheep. Among the Samburu, cattle represented the real wealth. One cow or bullock was worth ten or more goats and dozens of sheep. Through years of successful calving, the father of the family had acquired status in the Lbaa clan second only to the head elder. When three more young animals were born to his cows, the father would be able to afford his sixth wife. The head elder had but seven.

As Firingin thought of the father, his watchful gaze changed to one of somber reflection. He had always obeyed the family's leader, but he could not bring himself to like him. Though others in the family openly disliked the father because of his lack of generosity and his detached attitude, Firingin had a special reason for resentment.

It was the father who, nearly ten years earlier, had agreed to a tribal decision that condemned Firingin, the eldest son of his number-one wife, to life as a perpetual child. The father had stubbornly refused to take a clan challenge of Firingin's right to pass into Samburu manhood to a tribal council, and now Firingin, at twenty- two years of age, remained outside the society of adult males. Every day, he labored as a herdsboy, forced to do the chores of girls and small children.

A change in the sound of a nearby cowbell interrupted Firingin's thoughts. He turned his head and saw the lead cow and a half-dozen others loping toward the hilltop. While he'd been thinking of the father, they had made their break for the green grass on the opposite slope, grazing that was reserved for the head elder's animals.

Firingin scrambled up the incline. If the beasts succeeded in their escape, he would face public ridicule in the village courtyard. The father would face embarrassment before the elders, and that would bring instant condemnation to his eldest herder.

As Firingin neared the top, he looked for the girls and the small boys who were supposed to help. They were nowhere in sight.

It was not fair. Why could they always slip from their duties and never face punishment? The father never expected anything from them. Why should he? He had an adult herding his beasts.

Firingin reached the crest and saw a pair of the breakaway animals already racing along the rocky crown.

He turned and ran in front of their charge. He knew they would not descend to the grassy side until the lead cow reached the top and showed the way. The lead cow and several young bullocks climbed up a lower trail. Her massive, white body knotted and extended on the hillside just below Firingin.

His lungs burned, but he forced his legs to move faster. He must not let the leader of the revolt beat him to the crossover. He shouted her name, but it didn't distract her. With a frantic lunge that scraped one of her horns against a rocky outcropping, she jumped ahead.

Firingin had one weapon left. He stopped and scooped up a handful of pebbles.

The lead cow, like all livestock in Northern Kenya, survived among stealthful predators by quick reactions to sounds at ground level.

He threw the stones directly in front of the animal's flared nostrils. The barrage hit, and she shied. With eyes bulging, she lunged down the dry side of the hill. The others dutifully followed the sound of retreat from her bell.

Firingin stood on the crown, breathing hard. The breeze above the dusty ravine felt cool against his sweat-covered skin.

He heard bells on the grassy slope where the cattle and goats of the head elder's herd grazed and saw some of the young herders stop their work and point up the hill. The shrill sounds of their ridicule rose with the gusts of wind.

He shook his head. Those children jeered, but they knew nothing. They hadn't even been alive when his shame had started.

He had then been ten years of age and had just returned to the village after his first year at the Kenyan School. He'd been the only one from the clan to ever go to the school, so he'd instantly become the center of attention in the courtyard. The Lbaa people had watched with glistening eyes when he'd shown them his books. They'd listened with rapturous attention while he'd told about the arithmetic and the Swahili language he'd learned.

For over a week, the time had been joyous for him. Then, the beginning of his trouble appeared.

He had awakened for what he'd expected to be another happy day and had gone to relieve himself. It was then he'd noticed that his foreskin had partially grown shut.

It seemed a strange affliction but one he had thought would soon disappear. He'd tried to ignore it, but the next time he'd gone to pass water, the skin had nearly closed. Embarrassed, he'd told no one. The growth continued, and after several days, no matter how much he strained, he had not been able to urinate.

He'd grown hot with fever. On the third morning, he'd lain on his bedmat, unable to get up, and his mother had squirted water on him. The fever got stronger.

Then his mother had stated her conclusion that he must have caught the illness at the Kenyan School and that the doctors at the school's clinic had to be the ones to treat the affliction. She'd followed that proclamation with an order for Firingin's younger brothers to carry him to Maralal.

By the time the procession had completed the daylong trek, Firingin had become unconscious. Surgery had been performed immediately, and the traditional act of circumcision, reserved by the Samburu for the initiation of a boy into manhood, had been preempted by a Kenyan doctor. Firingin had never even seen the knife. When he'd awakened from the anesthetic, he'd discovered his unearned symbol of adult status already in place. Soon it brought him a life of shame, an existence filled with the laughter of ridicule.

An up-slope breeze brought the bawling sounds of the father's cattle to Firingin's ears. Turning his back on the jeers of the head elder's children, he descended the hillside toward his charges.

Near a pool where the lead cow drank, Machyana, one of the missing helpers, sat on a shaded rock. The nearly adult son of the father's number-four wife gazed dreamily at the distant horizon.

Firingin felt fury grow in his chest. He slid in an avalanche of loose gravel toward the boy. "Why do you sit while I alone must stop the father's beasts?" he asked.

Machyana slowly turned his face toward the question. "I do not see a problem," he said. He smirked and pointed to the obvious. "The beasts graze contentedly."

"Don't tell me you didn't see the stampede."

"I saw it, but you ran ahead of the animals," Machyana said. "Everyone knows Firingin is the most experienced herdsboy in the Samburu tribe. Why should I worry?"

"I only stopped them by a lucky throw of pebbles. If I had not been so fortunate, the father would have faced embarrassment before the elders."

"And Firingin would have been chastised in the courtyard," Machyana said. He smiled. "But such things don't concern me." The boy stood and pushed out his chest. "When twenty more full moons have shown, I will become a candidate. Then I will herd these cattle no longer."

"Already you do not herd these cattle," Firingin said. He leaned over and stared into Machyana's eyes.

"Do you know where the girls and the other small boys have gone?"

Machyana's face showed anger at having been classified a small boy. He started to walk away, but Firingin grabbed his shoulder.

"They have gone where they always go," Machyana said. His eyes glared. "Or don't you even know where that is?"

Sweat oozed over the ridge of Firingin's eyebrows, and he stretched nervously to his full two-meter height.

Of course he knew. They went to Kisima Village, but he did not understand why. It did not make sense that the girls wanted to go there and show their bodies to tourists. The few shillings they received from the leering foreigners with cameras did not justify the disgrace.

"I must go for them," Firingin said. "The beasts will try again, and next time we might not be so lucky."

He pushed his reluctant half brother toward the animals. "Even you can watch the cattle now," he added. "As you say, they graze contentedly."

Machyana ambled toward the slope, and Firingin watched him leave. The boy was a forearm's length shorter than he, yet Machyana would soon be a lmurran, a warrior. The boy would become a man while Firingin, the true eldest son, would remain with the girls and the small ones. He ran his hand under his loin wrap and felt where the foreskin should have been for his own day of manhood.

Why had his mother not let him die?

He looked at the sun's ball halfway up from the horizon and started toward Kisima. He must hurry.

Machyana could not be trusted with the animals for long.

Leslie Halstrom straightened her back to relax its muscles. For nearly an hour, she had worked in the morning heat, and still she had several things to pack.

It would be sad leaving Lake Barringo's Island Camp.

She would miss the lush greenery and adorable African children, but she looked forward to the photo safari's next stop. The Samburu Reserve would bring back the game drives.

Leslie loved seeing the elephants. She delighted in the way the giant females always placed themselves between the babies and danger. Some people in the tour group complained when the little ones were hidden from the cameras by adult legs, but not Leslie. Without a family of her own, she admired the way elephants in a herd cared for each other.

She took her Aunt Jean's photograph from the nightstand and placed it in her suitcase. For a moment, she regarded the poised countenance in the framed portrait and felt a familiar twinge of grief. Two summers had passed since her aunt had died, but Leslie still couldn't accept the loss. Aunt Jean had been everything to her—mother, father and best friend. For twenty years after Leslie's parents were killed in a car crash, Aunt Jean had been her family. In the days after the accident, Leslie, an only child, had withdrawn into a state of sullen detachment. Even now, she remembered the feeling. It had been as if she'd done something terribly bad and had been punished by having her parents taken away. In her Aunt Jean's home, the morbid feelings had continued, but the supportive atmosphere there had helped Leslie to recover. A self-reliant and caring strength had radiated from Aunt Jean. With her aunt as an example, Leslie had developed enough self-esteem to become an accomplished, if not socially talented, student in both high school and college.

After high school, Leslie had lived away from her aunt, but she'd stayed close through weekly telephone conversations and frequent visits. When the heart attack took its toll, Leslie had suddenly felt alone and once again felt as if she'd been punished.

A wheezing started in her throat. She stopped her work and walked to where the tent opened toward the lake.

A breath of fresh air might prevent the congestion from becoming a full-scale attack.

Dust was the worst part of the trips she'd started taking to help fill the void in her life. The airline tickets and tour expenses had used most of her inheritance money, but they'd been worth the price.

Strange lands filled with exciting people and natural wonders had provided sanity-saving distractions from those earlier feelings of melancholy.

Except for the first summer when Leslie had stayed

home—nobody could have traveled so soon—she'd gone overseas on packaged tours. No one would ever replace Aunt Jean, but Leslie had found comfort traveling with women from her age group. On last year's trip to China and on this one to Kenya, Leslie had traveled in the company of a fellow faculty member from Cleveland's King Middle School. At thirty-two, Leslie was more than ten years younger than most of her teacher-colleagues, so she'd had little trouble finding suitable candidates.

At the tent opening, she pulled back the flap and took a deep breath to clear her lungs. She squinted at the scene outside and growled as she reached in her handbag for her glasses. She hated wearing them, but her contacts were soaking to remove a stubborn speck of what must have been mold.

She put on the horn-rims and perceived a flock of turquoise finches and yellow sunbirds flitting over the broadleafed foliage. She enjoyed the African birds. Even the starlings were pretty.

Below the camp area, the muddy waters of Lake Barringo lapped against the shore. Leslie looked for the boat that would take the tour group to the mainland. Evidently it hadn't arrived. Footsteps approached the tent at the opposite end. Leslie removed her glasses and turned around.

Mary Osborn ducked through the doorway. She was this year's traveling companion and the woman who shared the sleeping quarters with Leslie.

"So, here you are," Mary said. "I was beginning to get worried."

Leslie smiled. Mary was the best possible vacation partner. At fifty-four, she was old enough to be physically like Aunt Jean and she was almost as self-assured and resourceful.

"You've missed breakfast, you know," Mary said.

"I've been packing. I didn't want to be late."

"Well, you won't be late, that's for sure. They just announced in the dining hall that there has been a change of plans. We won't be leaving for another hour."

"Wonderful," Leslie said. "I'll use the time for a quick trip back to the Njemps School."

"That's a superb idea," Mary said. She stepped back and beamed at Leslie. "You know, I don't believe I've ever seen you happier than you were yesterday. Those little ones really turn you on, don't they?"

Leslie nodded. "They were darling. With students like that, I think I could actually enjoy teaching again."

"Don't even mention teaching," Mary said. "Four weeks away from the King Middle School, and I'm only now getting back to being human."

Leslie selected the blue hair clip from her jewelry box. It was the best color to bring out the gold of her unruly hair. She snapped the clip around her ponytail and picked up the bag of plastic toys she'd brought for the native children.

"Why don't you come with me? Together, we could still pass these out."

"Can't—got all my packing yet to do."

Mary touched Leslie's sleeve. "Don't you have anything lighter to wear?"

"Why can't I wear this? It's all I have that's clean."

"Well, you might cook. Calvin, our ever-faithful guide, said we'll be going through some hot country today."

"Even hotter than usual?"

"I guess so. He said because we're getting such a late start, the tour company is taking us on a shorter route. We'll be going through an arid region north of here."

"Won't we get to see that Rift overlook?"

Mary shook her head.

"Damn! And I wanted so much to see it. Ever since *Out of Africa*, I've been wondering how it would look."

"If it makes you feel any better, you're not the only one who's upset. As soon as Calvin made the announcement, Phillis Manning let out a groan. You should have seen George laugh when she started complaining about not getting to see where Robert Redford was buried."

Mary kicked out of her denim skirt and looked over at Leslie. "You need to get a move on if you want to see those children."

"I won't be able to now," Leslie said. "I have to unpack all my stuff to find some shorts and a halfway clean T-shirt."

"Get changed, then," Mary said, "When we're packed, we'll go up to the bar and cool off." Mary selected a sleeveless blouse from her suitcase. "Oh, Leslie," she added, "guess who I saw sitting there all by himself?"

Leslie shrugged.

"Brian Westerson. And Kimberly was nowhere in sight."

"Mary!" Leslie said. "Why do you always think I'm interested in people like Brian Westerson?"

"Well, aren't you? Without the competition?"

Leslie looked down at the two, barely perceptible bulges in her blouse. For her, there would always be competition. "I don't think it makes any difference what I think," she said.

Mary shook her head, and Leslie retreated to the bathroom. She busied herself inspecting the contacts.

It was painful for her to even think about men. Throughout her life, they'd made her feel uncomfortable or worse.

Living with an unmarried aunt, Leslie had rarely been around adult men as a child. At school, her experiences with boys, except for one little black boy who might have liked her, had mostly been painful. As the recipient of their taunts, she'd grown fearful and shy. In high school, Leslie had been slow to develop physically. She'd been even more skinny then than now.

She'd resorted to books for comfort. The boys in high school had avoided her.

She tried a dorm party or two when she first started at Ohio State. Living on her own, she'd fantasized beginning a new social life. The few men who attended the parties had seemed almost as inhibited as she, and the ones in her classes all seemed to be going steady. In her junior year, Leslie's roommate had once invited her to double date. Though she'd never met the man, Leslie had enthusiastically accepted. They'd gone to a movie, a good one, *The Sting*. But, Leslie had been so tense over being out with a man, she hadn't been able to follow the plot. On the way home, her date, who had said nothing to her after hello, had suddenly become amorous. In the back of the car, without saying a word, he'd started pulling at her blouse. She valiantly fought him, but probably wouldn't have been saved from being raped if he hadn't ejaculated prematurely. It had been her last college date. Her roommate had never asked her again.

After graduation she occupied herself with her teaching career. There had been few men at her school, and the ones there had been either married or too old.

She wasn't the type to go to singles bars or even to take the initiative with the one or two potential dates at her church. Years passed without any close contacts.

After Aunt Jean died, Leslie had become so lonely she took the advice of the church minister and joined the singles group. After several meetings, she met an older man who seemed kind and considerate. She talked to him several times, and because he also seemed lonely, she'd taken the initiative and had invited him to her apartment for dinner. She prepared her specialty, lasagna, and after they enjoyed the meal, she put a Vivaldi tape on the stereo. They settled on the sofa to listen to the music. She might have been expecting too much, but she liked the man and had hoped that, perhaps, something would happen. The something that did happen had been the music had triggering him to start talking about his estranged wife and his children.

Leslie had listened with interest at first, but soon she discovered that the man's main interest was to return to his family. That had ended her only attempt at a serious relationship.

The water running in the sink brought Leslie back to reality. She turned it off and placed her contacts in her eyes. When she returned to the main part of the tent, Mary was already packing.

* * *

As casually as possible, Leslie bent over to lift a valise to the top of the bed.

A blue and orange lizard scuttled from where it had been hiding under the end table, and Leslie jumped. The creature scampered to a new hiding place, and Leslie looked at Mary. "I hate those things, don't you?"

Mary smiled and pulled an armload of clothes from her closet.

Leslie was still looking for the t-shirt when Mary finished packing. The older woman stood for a moment and watched. Then she lifted the front of her blouse away from her body. "It's too hot in here," she said.

She stared into her pocket mirror, and tucking her lips to even an application of lipstick, she turned toward the doorway. "So I guess I'll go on ahead."

Leslie was pleased that Mary hadn't said any more about Brian Westerson, but knew she'd been looking forward to the bar. "Sure," Leslie said. "Go on. I'll be awhile, and actually, I want to read a little in my guidebook. There's a section in it about the elephants of the Samburu Reserve."

Mary nodded. "See you on the dock then."

Leslie had been taking deep breaths of fresh lake air to clear her lungs while she watched the boat pull up to the finger pier. She hadn't noticed that Owen Polier had sidled his blimpish hulk beside her.

"So Leslie, are you ready for a hot trek today?" he said. "Or didn't you hear about it?"

She looked at him but didn't answer. Owen's condescending attitude didn't deserve a response.

"I saw you weren't at breakfast this morning," he persisted. "Getting your beauty sleep, were you?"

"I wasn't asleep," she snapped. "Not everyone is a perpetual eating machine like you, Owen."

He leered. "My, aren't we touchy today. What's the matter, Leslie? Pissed over missing Robert Redford's grave?

Or is it your time of the month?"

She felt like punching his enormous stomach but decided instead to move. She leaned over to pick up her suitcase and then felt his pinch on her behind.

Of all the men in the world, Owen Polier was the last she would allow to take such liberties. "Knock that off, you creep," she hissed. She swung her handbag, narrowly missing his groin.

A crooked grin crept over Owen's face, and he shifted his weight as if to grab her.

Suddenly, Johanna, the tour guide's wife, stepped from behind Leslie. She faced Owen for a long moment and then turned around.

"My word, Ms. Halstrom," she said, her eyes smiling. "That's quite a swing you have. An inch higher and this poor man might have been crippled for life."

Leslie started to laugh but stopped when she saw Owen's eyes. The fire of pure hatred now burned behind them.

Johanna turned back to him. "As for you, Owen," she said, "you might try doing something useful with all that energy. Calvin would be ever so grateful for a little of your help loading the luggage."

A few minutes later the fifteen-meter, motorized canoe with its cargo of chatty tourists putted out on the calm waters of Lake Barringo. A breeze wafted back from the forward motion, and Leslie made an effort to keep her face toward it. Her attack of congestion hadn't yet subsided.

She and Mary had boarded the dugout last and were seated in the back row—Leslie on the outside. From her position in the backward facing seat, she looked directly at one of the nearly naked Africans who helped run the boat.

She tried to keep her eyes from him, but he was immediately in front of her. One of the times when she turned back from the breeze, she saw him looking.

He smiled, and she felt her face redden. She looked aside but, after a moment, glanced back. He was young and physically attractive, but she couldn't get over his eyes. Deep and brown, they gazed at her from his black face and exuded a tenderness she'd never seen before from a man. Several times after that she looked at the boatman, and each time his eyes were the same.

Suddenly, a squeal came from the front of the canoe. The tour group's party girl, Kimberly, had spotted a herd of hippos at the edge of the lake. She stood up on her seat and started giving reports to the passengers. The boat rocked, and Brian Westerson wrapped a protective arm around her thighs.

Feeling embarrassed at the sight of Brian and Kimberly nearly making out in front of everybody, Leslie intently scanned the horizon with her binoculars. Near the shore, she saw the backs of the dark animals in the water.

Kimberly continued her animated observations until the hippos slipped out of sight. After she finally sat down, Owen made one of his attempts at humor by complaining loudly that he'd missed seeing the hippos because he'd thought Kimberly had wanted people to watch her hips roll.

The passengers grew silent, and the canoe continued its journey. When the boat entered a large bay on the mainland side of the lake, the African in front of Leslie jumped from his perch and started shouting.

Calvin interpreted his Swahili words. "He says that crocodiles are swimming between us and the shore. Everyone should look where he's pointing."

Leslie's face was about a foot from the boatman as he turned toward the water and then back to Calvin. She tried to look for the crocodiles but felt herself grow faint. The smell of the man's obviously unwashed body was overwhelming.

She leaned toward the side of canoe and grabbed the gunwale for support. The boat rocked, and her hand slipped.

She saw the water coming up to meet her, but an arm moved to block her fall. She was pushed back, and then she saw the face with the arm. The boatman's eyes were there, looking at her.

"Are you all right?" Mary asked.

Leslie held onto her companion. "I just couldn't breathe for a moment."

"I tried to grab you," Mary said. "What in the world happened?"

Leslie nodded toward the native who now sat on the boat's transom. "I've never been able to tolerate strong odors." She released her grip. "I think I'm OK now."

Mary patted Leslie's shoulder. "Yes, I noticed the smell too," she said, "but isn't he fantastic to look at?"

Leslie didn't answer.

After a time she felt the boatman's eyes on her.

She felt them, and finally she looked. There they were, sadly gazing across the short distance. She smiled, but that time the African looked away.

When the tour group disembarked on the mainland side of the lake, only one of the vans had arrived.

"Sammy says the other van will be here shortly," Calvin explained. "Johanna will take you first seven and go on ahead. The rest will wait and come later with me."

"We'll probably be separated for the entire trip," he added. "There are different routes across the region. But, don't worry, we'll all make it to the lodge in time for our afternoon tea. After that, we'll have a few hours left for an evening game drive."

Leslie smiled at the thought of seeing the animals, and she looked around to see who would be with her in the first van. There was Mary, of course, and, unfortunately, Owen. Phillis and George Manning followed them up the ramp, trailed by the seventy-five-year-old twin sisters from Moline, Illinois. Everyone knew the sisters' age because the group had given them a birthday party last Tuesday.

The sisters struggled into the van first and took the seat in back of the driver's. Leslie took the window seat behind them, and Mary sat next to her. The Mannings climbed into the rear, and Owen settled his mass on the shotgun seat in front.

Johanna supervised the loading of luggage and climbed into the jump seat behind Owen.

Finally everything was ready, and everyone applauded—everyone except Sammy. Their usually cheerful driver seemed apprehensive as he slammed his door and started the engine.

As the van bounced out along the dirt road north of the lakeside village, the riders were unusually quiet. Everybody must have been exhausted from their packing.

George Manning fussed over his cameras. "Calvin told me we might see camels on this leg," he said. "That's about the only kind of animal I haven't gotten a shot of."

Johanna turned around in her seat and corrected him in her matter-of-fact way. "We still haven't seen the gerenuk, the reticulated giraffe, and Grevy's zebra," she said. "We should see all of those in the Samburu Reserve. In addition, you may get to photograph the Samburu dancers at the lodge."

"This looks like a good time to load up, anyhow," he replied.

"I just wish we hadn't missed the Rift overlook," Phillis said. One of the sisters nodded.

Clouds of dust rolled in through Owen's partially open window.

"Can't you close that?" Leslie said.

Owen scowled. Johanna shook her head. Without saying a word, she reached forward and cranked up the glass.

Owen sat glumly quiet. He'd probably never speak to Leslie again, but that was fine with her.

The sisters started chattering to each other about the canoe trip. Raucous laughs punctuated their whispered comments about Kimberly's dance and about the almost naked boatman. One of them looked over the back of her seat at Leslie. There was a twinkle of mischief in her eye when she spoke. "He leaned way over when he saved you from falling in," she said. "Didn't you see anything?"

Leslie felt her face flush. "I didn't look," she said. Owen turned around and seemed ready to make a comment, but

Johanna held up her hand. "I think this has gone far enough," she said.

In the quiet that followed, Leslie thought about the serious-eyed African. She should have spoken to him. With her half-dozen words of Swahili, she could have at least said thank you.

By the quarter-way point, when the van was traveling east of Kinyang Village, the only travelers obviously awake were Leslie and Johanna. Leslie thumbed through her book about elephants, and Johanna stared at a paperback novel.

Everyone seemed to have gotten bored with the arid countryside. It was by far the driest part of Kenya they'd seen so far. All the places before had been at least partly green. The Masaai Mara had been surprisingly lush. In some places, the grass was tall enough to reach the shoulders of Thompson's gazelles and impala. In this northern country, such animals hadn't even been seen. The only creatures around in great numbers, other than native people, were cattle and goats.

Whenever there was a grove of trees, a bunch of cows or smaller animals would be crowded into the shade. Children were gathered around them, some solemnly watching the animals and others simply playing.

In one town, a group of skinny-looking men led a string of camels along a dusty street. The men, like most of the people in this region, looked as if they lived on the edge of starvation. Leslie wondered if it ever rained here. The real desert, the Sahara, couldn't be far away. Maybe the camels were from the Sahara.

On the rut-filled road, the van bounced up and down constantly, irritating, but Leslie had adjusted to the motion. She'd grown accustomed to the vertical jostling, but a sudden jerk in the vehicle's forward momentum caught her off guard.

"What was that?" she asked.

"I don't know," Johanna said. "Sammy, is anything wrong?"

"The engine coughed," he answered. "But now it's smooth

again. Maybe there was an air bubble in the petrol."

"Just keep it running," Johanna said. "We don't want to walk in this place."

Mary stretched and rubbed sleep from her eyes. Maybe the jerk had awakened her. George didn't seem to be bothered—he started snoring again.

"George!" Phillis snapped. "Stop that." The snores got louder.

When the engine sputtered the second time, Owen, who must have been awake all along, found his voice. "I think old George's snores must be scaring the life out of it."

"Funny, funny," Mary said. Owen smiled, but nobody laughed.

"What kind of natives were those we just passed?" Leslie asked Johanna. "The ones with the camels?"

"Njemps, I think. Or maybe Turkana," Johanna answered.

"I think those people are Rendille," Sammy said. "And they are far south. They must be looking for water."

"They looked like a bunch of beggars to me," Owen said. "What do they use camels for?"

"For transport of goods," Sammy answered. "Those carried empty water bags. Sometimes the Rendille use their camels to bring salt and other supplies from Ethiopia to villages in this country. They trade what they bring for water."

"The villages are supplied by camels?" Leslie asked.

Several of the towns the van had gone through had been jammed with hundreds of native people. She found it hard to believe that trains of camels could serve them.

"Some times of the year, it is the only way," Sammy said. "When the roads get wet, trucks cannot get through. They will try and that is what makes the ruts."

"Yeah, you'll probably have to take this van in for an overhaul after this," Owen said.

"Possibly," Sammy replied. Then, as if it wanted to provide corroborating evidence, the vehicle shuddered and the engine coughed to a stop.

Now even George was awake. "What the hell's going on?" he asked.

"Your snoring killed it," Owen quipped. Mary groaned.

Sammy took a look under the interior hood but evidently saw nothing unusual. He pulled a long-bladed knife from the glove compartment and laid it on the edge of his seat. As he reached for the door handle, one of the sisters leaned over and pointed at the knife.

"What's that for?" she asked. "I hope you don't expect any dangerous animals."

"Not for animals," Sammy replied.

The passengers watched, speechless, while their driver stepped out and made a circuit of the inert vehicle. When he returned, he said nothing. Solemnly, he took a small toolbox and his jacket from under the seat and disappeared beneath the van.

"He probably knows what's wrong," the more talkative sister said to her sibling. "I was scared at first, weren't you?" The other sister nodded.

"So, what is the knife for?" Owen asked Johanna.

He, like the rest of the group, seemed to consider the tour guide's wife the repository of all knowledge about Africa—even insight on the motives of their African driver.

In a hushed voice, Johanna answered. "I think he's worried about the natives in this area. I've noticed that he's been troubled ever since we loaded up this morning."

"But he's a native himself," Mary said. "Doesn't he know how to get along with them?"

"He's Kikuyu," Johanna answered. "His tribe is pretty much made up of city dwellers and farmers. The natives around here are nomads and scavengers. Some are worse."

"Now I'm scared," Phillis said.

Sammy climbed back into his seat and tried the van's starter. After a few turns, the engine thundered to life, and everyone cheered.

Johanna leaned over the back of Sammy's seat. "Is it fixed now?" she asked.

"I drained some fuel from the line," he said, "but the problem could return. I will take the turnoff to the Maralal Game Sanctuary. If they don't have a mechanic, I will use their radio to get help."

"I don't want to second-guess you, Sammy," Johanna said, "but why not go directly to Kisima? They must have a service station there."

"There is no help in Kisima," he replied. "It is a settlement where the Samburu congregate."

"Well, do as you think best," Johanna said. She turned to the others. "Did anyone happen to grab some extra fruit at breakfast?"

The van seemed to be running well when Sammy took the Maralal turnoff. "It is only about thirty kilometers now," he said. Confidence had finally started to show in his eyes.

The road became smooth after it narrowed. Reduced truck travel off the main route must have cut down the ruts.

The scene alongside the road had changed. No more crowded towns with dusty streets and junky shacks. The terrain in all directions had become open savanna. Dried grass dotted with towering anthills and scrubby looking bushes covered the hills and valleys. Suddenly dik-diks and small herds of impala had appeared. The road must have entered the game sanctuary that Sammy had mentioned.

Apparently hoping to still make it in time for the afternoon tea, he pushed the speed to fifty kph. The highway dropped into the ravine for a small river, and the van went even faster. On the upgrade, it slowed a little.

When it reached the crest, it continued to lose speed. Sammy leaned over the steering wheel and pumped the accelerator. The engine sputtered, died, and coughed back to life.

The vehicle rolled slowly forward, losing momentum. The engine had gone completely silent.

Sammy tried a compression start. It didn't work.

The van coasted to a stop. Without a word, he went through the routine of placing his knife on the seat and getting out with his jacket and tools.

"Christ!" George said, "Now we're in the middle of nowhere, too."

This time Sammy stayed under the van for a long time. George speculated on causes of the trouble and got up from his seat. When he moved toward the door, Phillis jerked him back.

"George! Don't go out there," she said.

He grumbled and settled back in the seat.

Suddenly, Sammy climbed into the van and slammed the door. He had returned so quickly he hadn't brought his tools and jacket with him.

"Samburu!" he said. Keeping his hand behind the door, he hefted his knife to the ready position.

Leslie looked in the direction of Sammy's stare and saw two red-skirted youths standing beside the road.

Each of them held an eight-foot metal spear at his side.

Silently, they regarded the motionless vehicle.

"Warriors!" Johanna said.

"I kinda gathered they weren't kitchen maids," Owen replied.

"See the beads and how they have their hair matted down with ocher paste," Johanna continued.

One of the sisters waved through her window, and one of the youths grinned a toothy response.

Johanna leaned across to the sliding-glass that Leslie had opened a crack. She said something to the visitors.

The Samburu said something in return, but Johanna shook her head. "They don't seem to speak Swahili," she said. "Sammy, do you know any Samburu?"

"Only a few words," he answered. "But I do not think it wise to converse with them. And please, you must close the windows. They will steal things if they can."

Leslie suggested that Johanna try her Masaai. It had worked well with the natives in the Mara.

"These guys look like they're from the same tribe," George said.

"Looks and language are two different things," Johanna said, "but it's worth a try."

Sammy glared his disapproval when Johanna opened the window and spoke in the strange language. The taller, older-looking youth smiled and said a few words in return.

"I can't quite make out his dialect," Johanna said to the people inside, "but I think he's asked for food—candy maybe."

She spoke to the Samburus again, and quickly Sammy opened the door and scooped up his tools and jacket.

After he returned to his seat, he hit the starter.

The electric motor clicked and whined, but the engine remained silent.

The Samburus jumped and raised their spears toward the starter's sound. They looked at each other and then at the van. After a moment, they lowered their weapons and walked away.

Leslie watched them as long as possible, but it was only minutes before they disappeared.

Sammy sat with his head on the steering wheel.

For a time, no one spoke. Then Mary asked how far it was to the game sanctuary.

"About ten kilometers, isn't it, Sammy?" Johanna said.

"Maybe fifteen," he answered and tried the starter again. Again it failed.

"Wish I'd taken some pictures of those guys," George said. "Man, did you see them go for the spears?"

Leslie rubbed dust from her window and tried again to see the warriors. "I just wish I could have talked to them," she murmured.

3

The slap of Firingin's sandals on the hard roadbed broke the silence of the high desert. With three long strides, he crossed over the raised highway and slid down the embankment. Back in the bush, he ran with an even pace along the tribal trail. The pathway, smoothed by ages of travel between Samburu villages, provided a convenient route through the scrub forests and knife-edged grasses of the Lorogi Plateau. Before the sun glared from directly above, he would be in Kisima Village.

As he ran, he tried to think of words he would use to persuade the girls to return to their duties. It would take time to get them to come. He was glad he had stopped at the family's manyatta, the home village, and had sent three of the

father's smaller children to help Machyana.
   In mid-morning, the manyatta was a quiet place. The circle of dwellings that formed the commune for three families was nearly empty. A few penned up calves and a couple of sheep was the only livestock nearby. Firingin had gone to the dwellings where he knew small children stayed with their mothers. He'd told of the need, and the women had ordered their children to go. Every adult in the father's family valued the herd, but only children tended it. Across the manyatta's courtyard, Firingin had seen the father, sitting and talking with the other elders. Firingin had not spoken to him. It was best not to disturb the father's relaxation.
   Thinking of the punishment the father might administer, Firingin quickened his pace. The translucent ears of an African hare bobbed over the low vegetation beside the trail. His footsteps had frightened the rodent, but Firingin hardly noticed. Preoccupied with his mission, he ran by the animal, opening the black goatskin of his cloak to let the air cool his skin.
   A double flash of light winked from the ridgeline ahead. Firingin stopped behind a stand of thornbushes.
   The flashes winked again. A show of scarlet indicated that lmurran were present. They would not be Lbaa—the clan's warriors were on a cattle buying expedition to the South. Yet, it would be wise be avoid an encounter.
   Over the ten years since the father had given up on Firingin's right of passage, every Samburu in the region had heard of the shame. If Firingin were spotted by the lmurran on the hilltop, they would certainly detain him with games of harassment. He would wait a few minutes behind cover and save an hour of time.
   While he hid, he thought about the father's stubbornness and the way it had brought the shame of Firingin's premature circumcision before the entire tribe.
   It had happened during the weeks that followed the opening of that year's age-set. The call for candidates to become

Samburu men had been the first in over twelve years, and the father had waited long for the event. It was the age-set in which his first sons could start on the path that would make them warriors and potential recipients of cattle and goats through gifts and collected penalties. With the prospect for such an increase in family wealth at hand, he'd quickly named all of his eligible sons. Firingin and four others had been identified for the Lmugit, the initiation ritual. Even though Firingin's childhood surgery had been well known among the Lbaa, the father, in a fit of greed, had submitted his name for the circumcision ceremonies. The rules require the eldest son of a family to go first, and Firingin had been the father's eldest.

Firingin himself hadn't been consulted about the naming. If he had been, he would have agreed. His unusual badge of manhood had generated a measure of respect among his childhood peers. Becoming an initiate had promised to simply be a validation of the status he'd already achieved.

In the dwelling of Firingin's mother, it had been a time of celebration. She made the ceremonial black cloaks for him and for his younger brother. She and her household had looked forward with joy to their move to the Lorara, the ritual village.

Firingin had learned later that the clan elders had not been rejoicing. His candidacy had presented them with a potentially embarrassing problem. They reminded the father that no Samburu boy could enter the Lmugit unless that boy proves his courage against the blade.

Already circumcised, Firingin could not provide such proof.

The clan's elders had demanded that the father remove Firingin's name from the list. Initially, the father had refused. According to custom, the removal of his eldest would have also barred his younger sons. The elders had proposed an appeal to the Samburu council for their recognition of Firingin's prior circumcision. The father, fearing potential embarrassment before the high-level elders, had become furious. Shouting threats of curses on his clansmen, he had rejected their idea.

Though many have said that such appeals had been granted, Firingin's petition for entry into manhood was then dropped. After several days, the clan elders and the father had agreed to remove Firingin's name from the list of the father's male descendants and to declare Lawi, the father's next son, as his legitimate eldest.

During a short ceremony in the village courtyard, Firingin had been publicly designated a perpetual child and from that day to the present had been required to wear his black, ceremonial cloak. It had become recognized everywhere as his badge of disgrace.

Standing behind the clump of bushes, Firingin felt the sun's rays boring through the heavy goatskin of his garment of shame. He stepped from behind the foliage and scanned the horizon for signs of the warriors. They were not in view.

He started again along the trail, and after a short distance, he came to a small ravine. The sunken streambed extended in the direction of Kisima. He would use it to avoid further detection.

At first, he made good time in the ravine, but it narrowed, bringing thorns and jagged boulders close. His hidden travel became hard work, but he continued.

For nearly an hour, he climbed over rocks and squeezed through narrow openings. He wanted to sit and rest, but he could not take the time. Finally he stood on top of a large boulder and looked at the end of the canyon. After one more narrow passageway, he would be back in the open. Kisima would then be a short distance farther.

He pressed through the final crevice and then he saw them. Two lmurran stood in the pathway and held their spears as a barrier.

Firingin froze, and the warriors grinned.

He'd never seen these two before. Their dress, ochre paint, and jewelry followed the tradition of the Samburu, but their arms bore the scarring of the Turkana.

The taller warrior touched the fold of Firingin's cloak. "As we thought," he said to his partner, "he is the Lbaa herdsboy."

The other stepped forward and leered into Firingin's eyes. "And so far from his beasts," he jeered.

Their voices sounded strange. Firingin wondered if they might be from the clan that had migrated to the plateau from beyond the northern hills.

"Why do you travel here, herdsboy?" the tall warrior asked. "Is the child lost?"

These two might be new in the region, but they already knew how to enjoy his shame. He said nothing and cast his eyes about for a path of escape. He was one of the fastest runners in the tribe, and he did not believe that even primitives from Turkana country would throw weapons.

The walls rose sharply, and retreat into the canyon was impossible. The warriors would capture him at the first narrow passageway.

"The herdsboy is without a voice," the smaller warrior said. "Or maybe he doesn't know when he's lost."

"I am not lost," Firingin answered. "My travel is for the father of my family." He hoped that invoking the authority of an elder would frighten them into letting him pass.

"Oh, but you run so fast and so hidden, herdsboy. We thought you were fleeing from the thin-skinned tourists."

Firingin did not understand. "The tourists are in Kisima," he said.

"Today, tourists are behind you, foolish one. They and their Kikuyu are stopped on the road you crossed."

These must be the lmurran whose flashes he saw. They'd been running ahead of him since he left the bushes.

"You run in the wrong direction," the tall one said. "We have talked to your clan's people on the trail from Kisima and have told them about the thin-skins. Your helpers travel even now toward the road behind you."

They seemed to know everything.

Suddenly, the short warrior lowered his spear and with its tip, lifted the edge of Firingin's loin wrap.
Firingin stood still, furious but also terrified.
The muscles of his right arm tightened, but he resisted a move toward his knife. Jeers could be endured, a retaliatory thrust from a menacing spear could not.
Inside, he seethed with anger, but he said nothing. The uncontrolled nature of lmurran, when playing their taunting games, was well known.
"See," the short warrior said, "the herdsboy is as they say."
The other leaned over and stared. They both laughed.
"Perhaps his doctor made him to look like his Kenyan schoolteachers." They laughed again.
Suddenly, the lmurran tired of their sport. Perhaps they had seen the anger in his eyes. They looked at each other, stepped back a distance, and talked behind their hands. He could hear them speaking of the road and planning to return there. Then, without addressing him, they shouldered their weapons and pushed into the ravine.
He watched them go, trembling against his rage.
After a time, he decided to follow the warriors. If the helpers were on the road, as they'd said, he would have to risk more harassment from those primitives.
There was no choice.

The heat of the equatorial sun bore down on the metal shell of the tour van. The temperature inside had risen nearly ten degrees in the twenty minutes since the engine had coughed to a halt. The passengers campaigned for Johanna to open the sliding door, but Sammy refused.

"Those people will return," he said, "and they will bring others with them. We must not give them a way to get inside. And also we must never photograph them. If we do, they will demand money."

"Wait a minute, Sammy," George responded. "This is supposed to be a photo safari. How can you tell us not to take pictures?"

"You must not with these people," Sammy answered.

"But I'd be willing to pay for a shot of those guys with the spears," George replied.

"You do not have enough to pay them," Sammy said. "Once the Samburus see your shillings, they will want all you have. And they will take from the rest of us too."

"What a crock!" Owen interjected. "How can a couple of gussied-up bums take all of our money?"

Sammy didn't reply. He looked out the window for a moment before pulling a road map from the glove compartment.

"Shouldn't somebody start walking?" Mary asked. "We'll roast in here."

Johanna looked at Sammy and then at Mary. "I don't think Sammy wants to leave us," she said. "In this heat, I doubt that even he would make it. No, we'll just have to wait and hope that somebody comes along."

"If the warriors come back," Leslie said, "maybe we could somehow talk them into going for help."

"That's the dumbest thing I've heard yet," Owen said. "The heat must be melting your brain, Ms. Halstrom."

Leslie bristled but didn't say anything. What the heat had melted was Owen's short-lived visit to decent manners.

"Back off, Owen," Johanna said. "If the Samburu come back, I might take Leslie's suggestion. Help from the natives may be our only hope. I haven't noticed a single vehicle since we left the main road, have you?"

Owen shook his head.

"Eventually, Calvin will be sending out a search party," George said.

"Eventually," Johanna replied. She leaned over and tapped Sammy's shoulder. "We're going to have to open this door," she said. She tilted her head toward the sisters. "Some of the passengers could have health problems if we don't."

Sammy didn't answer.

"I'll stay by the opening to close it at the first sign of trouble," she added. She turned around and scowled at George.

"And I promise that nobody will take any pictures of the Samburu."

Sammy shrugged. Johanna leaned against the handle and pulled back the heavy panel.

One of the sisters clapped once when the door slid open, but nobody joined in and she stopped.

Everyone sat silent. Insect sounds from the otherwise quiet surroundings came through the opening along with the smell of dry grass.

Leslie hoped it wouldn't set off her congestion.

Sammy lifted the interior cover from the engine. He seemed to be acting out of desperation when he removed the air cleaner and examined the fittings underneath.

Owen shook his head in disgust. With the engine open, the shotgun seat must have become too cramped for his gigantic body. Without asking, he opened his door and stepped outside. Johanna opened her mouth, no doubt to order him back, but she closed it without speaking.

She probably realized that Owen wasn't likely to strike out in the bush on his own.

He looked once down the road and reentered the cabin through the side doorway. There was much grumbling on everyone's part as he made his way to the bench in the back. Both George and Phillis moaned when he crowded his bulk into their seat. Owen, of course, took the space by the window, leaving poor Phillis jammed between two sweating bodies—one large enough to fill half the seat.

"Do we have to put up with this?" George pleaded.

"For awhile," Johanna said. "Sammy can use more room to work."

"Just hope he knows what to do with it," George mumbled. The heat was getting to everyone.

The sisters whispered to each other, but no one else spoke. Leslie was grateful that the grasses were leaving her sinuses alone.

Suddenly, Phillis shrieked. "Look! More natives."

"Wow!" George said. "Now that's something."

Two partially naked young women approached the back of the van. Both had luxurious bosoms, covered only with thin layers of ocher paste. On their heads they wore bands of colored beads with shiny ornaments dangling toward their eyebrows. Neck rings made of numerous layers of beads were stacked from just above their breasts to the bases of their chins. Bright colored wrappings of cloth extended from their waists to about a foot above their sandals.

"No pictures!" Johanna commanded as several people reached for their cameras. "Don't even let them see your equipment."

With general grumbling, everyone obeyed.

Several children emerged from the bush. Some of them looked to be about ten or twelve, but a few were preschool age. The little ones scampered behind the women. They wore no clothes at all.

"Look at them," Mary said. "They don't even care."

Leslie longed to talk to them. She thought of giving out toys from her bag. It would be fun to see those little eyes light up, but she knew she wouldn't ask. Johanna would never allow it.

One of the women approached Owen's window, making camera-snapping motions with her hands. Johanna slid the door to within a few inches of closed. Sammy sat on his knees near the engine. He stared at the passengers.

Earlier, Leslie had seen him lay his knife on the seat.

The other woman moved close to George's window, also giving the picture-taking signals.

"Don't do it, George," Johanna said.

The woman moved in so close her breasts touched the side of the vehicle. Instantly, she jumped back, rubbing herself and scowling.

"She must have got her nippies burned," George said.

They all watched while the other woman inspected her companion and while the two women cautiously touched the van with their fingers. "They really must be backward not to know about hot metal," Mary said.

"They've probably never seen a van sitting still in the sun as long as this one," George volunteered. A rocket engineer, he had an analytical mind.

The little children were now at the crack Johanna had left in the door's opening.

"Close it, please," Sammy said.

"I will," Johanna replied, "but I don't want to crush their fingers."

"Soon they will be inside," he said.

Johanna waited and her patience paid off. The children left and ran toward the edge of the road. The two warriors had returned, and the small children clustered around them. The native women also went to the warriors. They talked, and then the entire group approached the rear of the van.

Johanna slammed the door.

The warriors along with the women and children assumed group poses, and the women kept making picture snapping gestures. Everyone inside the van just sat and watched. Sammy had made his point.

The heat inside the cabin had skyrocketed. "We'll die in here if we don't get air," Phillis said. She must have been nearly suffocating already with Owen wedged in beside her.

"They're too close," Johanna said. "Let's sit tight for a few minutes. Maybe they'll get discouraged."

Again patience was rewarded. After a few minutes, the women and the warriors walked to the edge of the road. They started talking and laughing as though the van with its encapsulated tourists had disappeared from the earth. Johanna opened the door, but it didn't make much difference.

Mary fished two apples from her purse and used her penknife to cut them into eight pieces. It might have been the heat making everyone giddy, but suddenly the group inside the van seemed to relax. The appearance of food, however meager, had brought forth a sense of community. One of the sisters passed around a half-roll of lifesavers, and Sammy pulled a canteen of water from under his seat and offered it to Johanna.

"For everyone," he said. "But please drink sparingly."

Several more children arrived outside the vehicle, but only one more adult. He was taller than either of the warriors, but he didn't have a spear. He had earrings and other jewelry, and instead of red, the cape he wore was black.

"What is he?" Owen asked.

"Another Samburu, I believe," Sammy answered.

"He must be some kind of a warrior," George said. "At least he has a knife."

One of the native women drifted toward the van, and the newcomer walked over to her. At once, they seemed to be in an argument.

"He must be a chief," Phillis said. "You see the way he's trying to boss that woman around."

"But she doesn't pay any attention," George replied. "She's turning her back on him and walking away. That guy's no chief."

Nearly ninety minutes had passed, and the temperature inside, even with the door open, had reached well above a hundred.

Two more warriors arrived. They stood by the road with the others and talked. The way they acted reminded Leslie of eighth-graders at her school. Showing off for each other seemed to be their main purpose in life.

Sammy told Johanna that he'd thought of something to check under the van. With uncharacteristic abandon, he grabbed his toolbox and dismounted.

One of the warriors saw him step out and raised a spear. Sammy didn't see the warrior. George started to move toward the door but stopped. Another warrior had pulled back the one with the spear. After a moment, sounds of clanking and pounding came from under the van.

Sammy was apparently ignoring the warriors who were

now embroiled in a heated argument. As the natives pushed and shoved each other, their group moved a distance away from the van. Their jostling and shouting was just like the vying for turf that Leslie, as a teacher, had seen so many times.

After a while, the warriors seemed to grow weary of the pushing and shoving, but they stayed behind the van and kept talking. Leslie stopped watching them and opened her book.

She sniffed. The membranes of her nose had started to swell. It must have been a congestive reaction to the heat agitated smells of the cabin.

"Johanna," she said.

The tour leader had been watching the children outside the van and rubbed her eyes as she looked back in the cabin.

Leslie waited until she stopped rubbing. "Since Sammy's outside, now," she said, "do you suppose I could step out too for a minute?" She sniffed to show how stuffed up she was. "I think I'll be in trouble if I don't get some fresh air."

Johanna looked toward the warriors for a moment and then scowled obvious disapproval at Leslie.

Leslie sniffed again. "I've been fighting this stuff all morning."

Johanna shook her head woefully. "OK, but stay close," she said. "First sign of any trouble, get right back in here."

Leslie grabbed a few toys from her bag. She couldn't wait to see the little Samburus' faces when she handed out the sponge footballs.

When she stepped out, it seemed that the total environment had changed—as if she were an astronaut stepping from a spaceship onto the moon. Even with people all around, it was a starkness that startled her.

As far as she could see, there was nothing but brush-covered plains and hills. She wondered briefly where these natives had come from.

Other than children, the only Samburus near her were an older boy and the man wearing the black cape.

The man looked even taller than he had from inside the

van. He and the boy stood several yards away and watched her with a curiosity she might have imagined coming from residents of another planet.

The small children seemed to accept her. As soon as she moved away from the doorway, they stampeded to her side. Hands out, they wanted the toys. She passed out what she had and went back for more. Mary handed out the bag.

An older boy and one of the native women came from behind the van. The boy approached Leslie, gesturing for a present. She resented his impatience but gave him one of the ballpoint pens. She thought of taking something to the boy beside the man in the black cape, but the man now looked angry.

Some of the small children ran to the native woman, and the space beside the van erupted with frenzied activity as one child and then another showed the woman their toys. It was wonderful to see how happy the gifts made them, but Leslie felt nervous about the angry man at the edge of the road. He had grabbed the boy at his side, and the boy had started struggling. Leslie considered returning to the van, but suddenly the man released the boy. She waited and felt better when the wide-eyed youngster approached her for a present. He seemed more polite than the other boy, so she decided to give him her special gift. She handed him the Cleveland Indians' ball cap, and he smiled. He didn't put it on but turned and walked toward the native woman, holding the bright-colored prize above his head.

The group of warriors and the other native woman stayed a distance behind the van. They'd become aloof or perhaps suspicious of all the wild activity. Leslie ignored them and kept passing out gifts until her bag was empty; one of the little boys then got the bag.

Suddenly a cheer went up from the direction of the warriors. The more playful native woman and the children had started tossing the sponge footballs back and forth.

Leslie stood near the van and watched. The game was

completely chaotic, balls and children everywhere. When one energetic heave sent an orange missile high over the young receiver's head and past Leslie, into the rough, she ran to retrieve it.

It had rolled under a bush, and when she leaned to pick it up, a flash of light swept by her face. She felt the rush of wind and jumped back.

Not more than four feet away, a long-bladed knife stuck in the ground. On one side of it squirmed the thick body of a dust-colored snake. On the other gaped the open mouth of the severed head!

She lost consciousness.

5

When Firingin reached the place where the tribal trail crossed the highway, he discovered a reason to appreciate the warriors. Their footprints turned onto the graded road and showed him the direction to his helpers.

He climbed out of the bush and sprinted on the thoroughfare until he spotted the tourist vehicle. It sat at the top of the hill on the far side of a shallow canyon. When he saw the white safari van painted with black stripes to look like a zebra, he felt a strange excitement. It had been months since he'd been close to any thin-skins. At the school, they had always been so interested in everything about him and his tribe.

A crowd of Samburus had gathered near the vehicle. Firingin counted twelve, the two girls and two boys from his

clan, the two warriors from the ravine, and six small children.
He frowned at the thought of dealing again with the lmurran. But he would not turn away. He'd come too far to leave without the others.

He ran the short distance through the valley and approached the van from the rear. As he drew near, he saw the faces of the tourists. They looked red, almost as if they wore ocher paste. He remembered the Peace Corps volunteers from the USA. Their faces had also turned red from the heat.

The van's Kikuyu driver sat in the front. Firingin thought of speaking to him but decided against it. Talking in Swahili would bring recriminations from the warriors. They had already poked fun at his schooling and would no doubt resent him conversing with an outsider in the language of the Kenyans. Like most Samburu, the warriors could be expected to ridicule anything that went beyond traditional teachings. If Firingin's mother, a Rendille woman, hadn't placed a special value on learning, he, himself, would not have gone to the government school. The father had objected, but Firingin's mother had beauty and held power over the father in those early days.

Firingin stopped on the side of the van opposite from the lmurran. He would wait there until one of his clan's people came close. Then he would attempt to persuade them to return.

He didn't wait long. Tillya, the older girl from the family, sauntered around the back of the vehicle, making picture motions at the tourists.

"Tillya, you must return to the cattle," he said. "Machyana now watches, alone with only the small ones."

"I'm not going," she said.

"But the father will be cursed if his beasts mingle with the head elder's."

"Why should I care about the silly old father?" Tillya said. "These tourists have shillings. The large one in the back likes me."

"But you must come," he said. She turned away and made

more picture-machine motions at the red face in the van's window.

Firingin's lack of status prevented him from grabbing her when lmurran were present. Seki, the other girl, stayed near the warriors. He would try to persuade Kissipan, the older of the two boys. In the past, Kissipan had always been the most attentive of the helpers.

Two more warriors arrived and started talking to the others. Firingin would wait in his place on the opposite side of the van.

Kissipan moved from window to window around the vehicle. He stood on his toes and looked in at tourists.

Firingin watched. When the boy came close, he would grab him and appeal to his sense of duty. The warriors would not care if he held the boy.

The Kikuyu came out of the van on the other side.

One of the new warriors stepped forward and raised his spear. The Kikuyu seemed intent on his work and did not look up. The tall warrior who had harassed Firingin in the ravine grabbed the new one's arm. The four lmurran joined in an argument. It was a distraction that Firingin could use. He pulled Kissipan to his side and spoke quickly.

"It is time to go," he said.

"I will not," Kissipan answered. "These tourists are strange creatures to see. I will stay and watch them."

Kissipan stretched his neck and looked over Firingin's shoulder. "Look at that one," he said.

Firingin turned around and saw that one of the tourists had stepped outside the big opening on the van.

"See. The tourist looks strange," Kissipan said.

The tourist did indeed seem unusual. Firingin could not be sure if it was a man or a woman. The chest seemed too flat for a woman but the hips were too broad for a man. When the tourist started handing out toys to the children, he decided it was a woman. Such an interest in young ones was like a woman.

Kissipan struggled to get away, but Firingin held his shoulder. "Do not disgrace yourself," Firingin said. "One as old as you should not beg for favors."

"I do not take orders from a herdsboy," Kissipan said. He thrashed about, but Firingin held on. The warriors remained distracted by their argument.

The small children started tossing the balls the tourist had given them. Seki joined them.

Firingin grew tired of holding his half brother. He released Kissipan and checked the position of the sun. He would return to the beasts without the helpers.

The warriors had come to watch the game. A loud yell came from them and the children. Seki had thrown the ball high over everyone's head. It landed beside the road, and the tourist ran toward it.

Firingin noticed a saw-scaled viper lurking in the shade of a bush, close to where the ball rested. The tourist had not seen the reptile.

Firingin's knife flew end-over-end—his throw an instinctive reaction. Snakes must be stopped before they tightened for their attack.

The knife swept past the tourist's face and decapitated the viper.

The tourist's skin turned pale, and she fell to the ground. She appeared to be dead, but Firingin knew she had only fainted. He'd seen a thin-skin visitor at the school faint at the sight of a small water snake.

He heard a shout from the van and saw the Kikuyu crawl from underneath. The man did not go to the tourist woman who had fainted. Instead, he turned to those in the vehicle. The Kikuyu also knew that the woman was all right.

The snake was dead, and the tourist would soon recover. Firingin could do no more, so he decided to leave. He took a step to retrieve his knife, but when he did, two of the lmurran ran past him. They went directly to the fallen tourist and threw a cloak over her face.

"What are you doing?" Firingin shouted. They didn't answer. Instead, they motioned Tillya and Kissipan to where the tourist lay and directed them to carry her into the bush.

"Don't take her away," Firingin screamed, but the Samburu paid no attention.

He started to chase them, but before he reached the edge of the road, he was grabbed from behind. He turned and saw the other two lmurran, the ones from the ravine.

"Stop them," he said. "They can't—" A blow to his back silenced the words.

"You have killed the thin-skin, herdsboy," one lmurran said. The other held Firingin's arm and pulled him toward the bushes.

"But she is not dead," Firingin yelled.

"Silence, foolish one," the warrior said. "We must leave this place before the thin-skins attack from their movable dwelling."

Firingin looked over his shoulder at the van. One of the men stood inside the big door and shook his fist, but the Kikuyu motioned the man back.

Firingin struggled for freedom, but the lmurran kept him restrained. They shoved him off the road and through an opening toward the tribal trail.

Leslie awakened to the most ghastly odor she had ever smelled, and her face was covered. She tried to move her arms, but people were carrying her!

"Put me down!" she shouted into the stinking cloth.

Nobody answered. She wiggled and squirmed her body, and the people dropped her. As she fell, the cover lifted from her face. She scrambled to her feet and looked at the people. They were the Samburu from the road, or at least some of them. From several yards away, they stared at her as though she were a ghost.

Leslie thought of the snake. One of the warriors must have killed it. But why had they moved her?

"Jambo," she said. The Swahili greeting seemed appropriate. She was acquainted with these people—visually at least. The Samburus jumped back at the sound of her voice. They seemed surprised that she could talk.

She looked around. The van was nowhere in sight!

She and the Samburus were in a small open area surrounded by high thornbushes. For some reason they had carried her from the road, but the van couldn't be far. She couldn't have been unconscious more than a few seconds.

"Van...ni wapi," she asked. The Samburus didn't respond to her awkward question about the van's location.

She stood and waited. She could yell for help, but that might scare the Samburu away. With things like snakes around, she didn't want to be left alone.

One of the warriors started shouting and pointing along the pathway. The other shouted back and gestured in the opposite direction. They acted like they were lost and couldn't agree on which way to go. They argued, shoving at each other and yelling. It was the same as back at the van. She wondered if Samburu warriors argued about everything.

After several rounds of pushing, the taller of the two broke off the dispute and came to Leslie. He shook his spear. She had no idea what he wanted and did nothing. He pushed her in the direction he seemed to want.

She walked, and he walked beside her. The other warrior followed several paces back, and the two women and the children trailed behind.

Leslie walked in silence, turning at intersections with other pathways according to the tall warrior's directions. She expected the van to appear at any moment and couldn't believe how far they had carried her.

The heat grew oppressive as the procession passed through areas surrounded by brush and dry grasses. They almost never broke into the open. The few times Leslie could see more than a few feet, she looked for the road.

She saw cattle in the distance and once a small herd of zebra but no sign of the highway.

Leslie's feet began to hurt. Her strap-topped sandals weren't designed for hiking.

A feeling of dread invaded her. What if they weren't taking her back? She looked at the somber native who walked at her side. He didn't seem hostile.

After a while, the leader signaled a halt. They were in another open area surrounded by high bushes.

Several pathways crossed the knee-high grass.

The warriors stood and gazed at an opening in the brush. Leslie also watched it. What else could she do?

Presently, three more Samburus appeared, the other two warriors from the van and the tall man in the black cape. One of the warriors walked behind the tall man and held a spear to his back. The tall man seemed to be a prisoner.

The new warriors and the two from the first group stood in a circle around Leslie and the tall man. The warriors talked, and again, there was much shouting and pointing in different directions. Leslie really began to wonder if they weren't lost.

The tall man tried to say something, but a warrior thrust the air with his spear and shouted. The man looked at the ground and stopped talking.

The conference ended, and the procession, with the three newcomers in the rear, marched out of the clearing.

The tallest warrior gave the directions. He was clearly the one in charge.

After walking another mile or more, Leslie knew that they couldn't be going back to the van. For some reason, she and the tall man were being taken as prisoners to a place deep in the bush.

As the realization hit her, Leslie shivered. Why were the Samburu doing this? The only thing she had done to them was to give a few presents to their children.

She wondered what awaited her at the end of the march. Would anybody find her out here? She wondered if any of the people in the van had tried to prevent her capture. Sammy might have crawled from under the van and brandished his knife, but he alone couldn't have done anything. Mary and possibly Johanna might have screamed for the Samburus to stop, but that would have been it—nothing from the rest. Owen had probably enjoyed the entire episode.

One of Leslie's sandals came unbuckled. She stumbled and almost fell. The lead warrior who was walking beside her held her by the arm. He then stopped the procession and waited while she fastened the buckle.

His kindness surprised her. She smiled to show her gratitude, but he seemed embarrassed and looked away. It was like the boatman all over again.

The column came to another clearing, and the two warriors with the tall man began shouting. Leslie's escort waved them forward. When they prodded their prisoner past Leslie, she saw the expression on the man's face. He seemed excited. His eyes were bright with emotion, and his jaw was set tight.

Maybe the man in the black cape wasn't a Samburu, and that was why they had captured him. If he were from another tribe, he might understand Swahili or even English.

She studied the tall form now trudging ahead and decided to try Swahili.

"Jambo, bwana," she said to his back. The muscles of his neck tightened, but he said nothing. Her escort waved his hand in front of her face and shook his head.

The column passed under a large acacia tree, and the lead warrior ordered a stop. A small stream seeped through the reeds beside the path, and some of the people took drinks from the water. Several of the men urinated near the tree. The Samburu did not seem to possess certain types of shyness. The women also relieved themselves, squatting alongside the trail.

At this point, Leslie was emotionally numb. She was tired, hungry and thirsty, and her body was covered with dirt from the trail. Her pain had blended into a single, dull throb that pounded behind her right temple. She stood rubbing her head and watching the Samburus as if they were images on television.

Her escort motioned for her to squat with the other women.

She shook her head. He laughed and beckoned to one of women, and she led Leslie to a place behind a bush. The woman nodded and pointed at the ground, but Leslie was too dehydrated to go—she'd had only one drink of water and a slice of apple since last night's dinner.

When the woman returned her to the warrior, he offered a drink from his jug. Leslie definitely needed fluid but the sour smell of his leather bottle nauseated her so much she had to hand the vessel back. Like everything around the Samburus, the bottle exuded the overpowering stench of spoiled milk.

The warrior shrugged and turned away. He shouted a string of words, and the marchers took their positions in the column. The procession started moving on the trail, and Leslie, once again, found herself trudging along toward somewhere.

7

When Firingin felt the jab from the sheathed point of the warrior's spear, he wanted to turn and kick the fool who had delivered it. It had hit the same place in Firingin's back where all the previous jabs had hit. The warriors who marched him as their prisoner were men without honor.

"What you do is not wise," he muttered.

The warrior answered with a jab.

"They will come for her."

"Quiet!"

Firingin and his captors came to an open space, and the warrior in front raised his hand. On the far side of the clearing stood the group who had carried off the tourist. As Firingin had predicted, the woman had recovered.

"Now you see for yourselves," he said. "She is…"

"Go!" the warrior behind said and prodded him toward the waiting people. "We will talk to our comrades."

"You must take the tourist back!" Firingin said.

The lmurran paid no attention. He pushed Firingin to a place beside the tourist. The warriors stood around them in a circle and talked.

"This foolish herdsboy says we must return her," one of his captors said.

"He knows nothing," the tall one with the woman replied. "We cannot take her back. By now the Kikuyu has used his talking machine to call for help. The Kenyans will come with weapons. We would be captured and killed."

Firingin concluded that the two lmurran who had taken the tourist were also from the primitive clan.

They had no knowledge of Kenyans. The Kikuyu did not have a talking machine. He would not have looked so unhappy if he had.

"We have done nothing to hurt the tourist," the smallest warrior said. "Why would we be killed because of a simple mistake?"

"The risk is great," the tall one said. "We will seek the advice of our firestick elders."

The tall one seemed to be the launoni, the ritual leader of the warrior group. None but a leader would suggest approaching the clan's firestick elders, the powerful ceremonial advisers for young warriors.

Firingin addressed the tall lmurran. "Your time to safely return the woman grows short," he said.

"No talking, you," the warrior behind Firingin said, jabbing again with his spear.

"What will we do with this one?" the smallest lmurran asked.

"He must come with us," answered Firingin's guard. "He is the Lbaa herdsboy, the one who went to the Maralal School. He speaks the Kenyan language."

The leader nodded. "If we let him go, he could help the police find us."

"But won't the Lbaa elders curse us for holding one of their people?" asked the small warrior. He had more honor than all of the others.

The tall warrior from the ravine pointed to Tillya and the other helpers. "These are also Lbaa," he said.

"They come willingly and can take their herdsboy back when the danger has passed."

"No curse will come," Firingin's other guard said. "This herdsboy is a child. Elders do not waste curses over such as he."

"It is settled," the leader said. "We will take the tourist and the herdsboy to our village. There we will seek the council of our old ones."

The warrior leader formed the group into a column with Firingin and his guards at the rear. The procession marched toward the afternoon sun, and Firingin worried about the cattle. It could be after darkness before the lmurran released him.

Tillya walked in the group in front of Firingin. He spoke to her. "You must return to the beasts. Machyana does not know how to bring them to the manyatta."

"No talking!" the guard shouted.

"The girl is from my family," Firingin said. "I must give her directions."

Tillya turned around. "I do not take orders from that one," she said, "and I do not want him to talk to me."

The guard called to the leader and requested that he be allowed to move Firingin forward. When Firingin passed the tourist, he noticed her looking at him. He did not understand why she was so interested. After he walked ahead, she spoke to his back, using strange-sounding Swahili. He would not risk answering.

After the procession passed through a small grove of trees, the smell of smoke filled the air. It was a familiar odor to Firingin. It indicated that they were near a Samburu village. A group of people came along the pathway toward them, and several red-cloaked elders were in the group.

The warrior leader approached the elders. They were, no doubt, the firestick ones whom he wanted to consult about the tourist. The elders ignored the warrior leader and walked around Firingin and the tourist. None of them said a word until the one with the bird's-bill cap turned and faced the warrior leader.

"Why have you brought these persons to our village?" he demanded.

The warrior leader pointed to Firingin. "We thought the tourist woman had been killed by that one's knife, and we carried away her body."

Another elder pointed at the woman and showed his teeth with a grin. "But the woman walks."

"After we carried her, she recovered."

"How can that be?" the elder said. "I have lived many years and have never seen one person—not even a thin-skin—recover from death."

The warrior leader looked at the ground.

Firingin saw anger growing in the eyes of the elders. He would volunteer the explanation. "She was not dead. She only fainted."

"Who is this strange one?" the elder with the cap asked. "And why does he wear the Lmugit cloak?"

"He is the Lbaa herdsboy," the warrior leader answered. "He is the one who lives as a child."

The elder nodded. "I have heard of him."

The other elders stared at Firingin. Then one of them asked, "Why was he brought here?"

The short warrior answered, "Because he threw the knife at the tourist. And—"

"This is indeed strange," the elder with the cap interrupted. "A herdsboy who throws his knife at a tourist woman. Why does he attack a thin-skin?"

"The Lbaa herdsboy is known to be strange," one of

Firingin's guards replied. "He went to the government school in Maralal. He even speaks the language of the Kenyans."

"But why would he attack a tourist?"

"It was a snake," Firingin answered. "I threw my knife and killed a snake."

"Silence!" the guard shouted. He shoved Firingin aside and spoke to the elder. "We had to bring this herdsboy with us. If we had left him, his language would have allowed him to talk to the police."

"The police will come without any help from strange herdsboys," an elder in the back said. "The thin-skinned woman will be sought until she is found."

The elder with the cap stared at the warrior leader and then at his three followers. "You foolish ones have brought danger to our village. If you were of age, I would curse you all. But you are young and that protects you."

The elder turned his back on the embarrassed lmurran and regarded Firingin. "If you threw at a snake, why did the tourist faint?" he asked.

"She was near it," Firingin answered. "Thin-skins often faint when they see reptiles. I saw it at the Maralal School."

The elder smiled and nodded.

Suddenly the tourist sneezed. She sneezed again, and the warrior leader tried to stop her. The children laughed.

Firingin felt confident after the elder's smile and pointed to an opening in the brush where a fresh breeze ruffled the grass. The warrior led the woman to the place, and she stopped sneezing.

When the warrior brought her back, the woman spoke to Firingin. It sounded as if she said thank you, but he wasn't sure and didn't answer.

The crowd started to move toward the village, and Firingin asked the elder with the cap for permission to return to the cattle.

"We have need for your knowledge of thin-skins," the elder answered. "I cannot make you stay, but the tourist woman speaks to you. That could help us."

Firingin looked to the sky. It would soon be dark. Already the father will be angry.

Firingin wondered how grateful the elder might be if he helped with the tourist. If Firingin talked to her and that solved the primitive clan's problems, would the elder be willing to speak for him at the tribal council?

Firingin smiled. Perhaps a way to adult status had finally come to him.

He approached the elder with the cap. "I will stay," he said.

The elder smiled.

8

When Leslie saw the old men, she almost laughed. They all wore strange-looking hats. One had a tattered, New York Yankees' baseball cap on. Its bill was turned up the way little boys sometimes wear them.

Her warrior escort halted the column, and the newcomers crowded around Leslie and also the tall prisoner in the black cape.

The old men studied Leslie with serious eyes and spoke in terse sentences to her escort. The tall prisoner talked to the old one with the ball cap. Unlike the warriors, the old man seemed to listen to him.

The children laughed and pointed at Leslie. It was as if she were some kind of freak in a sideshow. Maybe that's why she'd been captured—to entertain their children.

Inside the circle of Samburus, Leslie's breath grew short. Suddenly she sneezed.

The Samburus jumped. She sneezed again, and her warrior escort held his hands in front of her face. He must have thought that would stop her. It didn't. The smell of him so close produced an even more violent explosion. The natives laughed, and the warrior looked embarrassed.

Through watery eyes, Leslie saw the tall man point to a breezy opening in the surrounding brush. The warrior nodded and led her to the fresh air.

It had the desired effect, and Leslie smiled to show her gratitude to the tall man. He didn't react.

"Asante sana," she said. The familiar Swahili expression of thanks drew a direct look from him, but he said nothing.

Leslie's warrior escort directed her along the widening pathway, and after a short walk, they reached a large clearing. On the opposite side, a busy native village, probably the column's destination, sat under a canopy of tall, spreading trees. The village was a collection of about twenty dome-topped huts, surrounded by a high barricade made of brambles, much like the Masaai villages the tour group had passed near the Mara.

Dozens of people rushed through openings in the village's barricade and ran directly across the field toward Leslie. News of her arrival must have spread to the entire community. Like the people on the pathway, these natives gathered around Leslie and stared. Her escort tried to wave the gawkers away, but they wouldn't go. They pointed at Leslie and the children laughed, but this new group completely ignored the tall man. He kept walking, now a distance away, with the old men.

Beyond the circle of gawkers, the scene was as alien as any Leslie had ever seen. Samburus and their animals were everywhere—like a Texas cattle ranch.

She took note of the lengthening shadows. The busy activity she saw could have been the village's evening roundup—she'd heard that Africans brought their livestock in each night for safety. Young Samburus, boys and girls still undistracted by her arrival, urged herds of cattle, goats, and sheep across the wide areas surrounding the settlement and toward the several openings in the stick and bramble fence. Whistles and shouts filled the air and enveloped each group of animals. Some of the livestock were already inside the compound. A chorus of bawling could be heard, presumably from the pens where the creatures were kept.

Leslie's warrior escort had managed to break the circle of spectators. He hurriedly led her across the field and through one of the openings in the barricade.

Inside the high fence, people again surrounded Leslie.

The warrior fiercely shoved them aside to clear a path and took her directly to one of the village's huts. His face looked angry. Since talking to the old men, the warrior had seemed upset with everybody.

In front of the hut, he growled something and pushed Leslie's face toward the opening.

Without thinking, she screamed. What she saw was dark and forbidding, like the inside of a Vietnamese hovel for prisoners she'd seen on TV.

The warrior shoved her through the doorway and stood outside while she picked herself up from the dirt floor.

Her head banged against the ceiling and she fell back. Tears from pain and anger filled her eyes.

After a while the warrior sat down by the doorway, and Leslie curled up on the floor. She tried not to cry out again. She'd always heard that it was best not to show emotions in violent situations. Throughout her life, lonely as it had often been, she'd never before felt so completely abandoned. When she'd lost her parents there had been Aunt Jean. Even when Aunt Jean died, she'd had colleagues and her work. Now she had no one at all to turn to.

She closed her eyes to block out the reality, but it was all around her. The sounds, the smells, and the overwhelming sense of hopelessness kept intruding until, finally, her exhaustion took over, and she slept.

Some time later she was awakened by a nudge at her shoulder. A woman leaned over her and held out a bowl.

Leslie sat up. The woman smiled and stirred the mixture. She offered a spoonful.

Leslie's stomach rebelled. It had been so long since she'd eaten, the walls must have been touching.

Yet she had to eat. The zigzags of hypoglycemia had already been streaking through her vision.

She tasted the offering. It was honey.

The woman handed her the bowl and the spoon. Leslie dipped up some of the contents, and then she saw the dead bees. Their bodies were folded into the honey, like raisins in cereal. She choked and handed the bowl back.

The woman wouldn't take it. She kept nodding and smiling. Leslie started to eat. Carefully she sorted out the bees before each mouthful. The woman watched.

She took the bowl when Leslie finished and handed her another. It contained water. Leslie drank; she had to have liquid.

After a few minutes, the woman left and Leslie crawled to the doorway.

The crowd outside had dispersed, but the warrior still sat at the post by the door. He was apparently there to guard her, but he seemed preoccupied and paid little attention to his prisoner.

The central courtyard of the village churned with activity. Even in her desperate condition, Leslie found it fascinating to watch. Women and young girls milked cows and goats in front of many of the other domed huts.

Old men sat in groups and talked, and young boys herded calves, small goats, and lambs from pen to pen. It was hard to believe that such a place actually existed in the late twentieth century. What stories she would tell if she ever got out of here!

She looked back into the hovel. The place smelled horrible. Like the other dwellings of the village, its roof appeared to be plastered with animal excrement. The odor of cow manure was everywhere.

The hut's rectangular interior was the size of a small bedroom in an American house. The corners were rounded, and there were no windows or doorways except the one in front. In the middle of the floor was a fire pit, and above was an opening for smoke to escape. Sticks of wood, probably for fuel, were piled near the entrance where Leslie crouched. Animal skin robes, thrown on both sides of the hearth, were no doubt for beds. There were no utensils of any kind except a few jugs.

One of the jugs exuded a particularly rotten smell, and Leslie crawled to pick it up. Before it made her sick, she would toss the putrid thing outside. When she grabbed it, the tippy vessel fell over and a dark, clabbered mixture flowed out.

Leslie choked back her nausea and watched the liquid soak into the dirt. She flicked dust over the stain and crawled back to the doorway.

It grew dark outside, and she slept in catnaps.

Once she was awakened when she heard a man talking to the warrior. It was the old man with the ball cap.

He spoke sharply, and the warrior looked worried.

After the old man left, the warrior laid on his side and looked unhappy.

Leslie watched from the shadows, and after a few minutes, the man with the cap returned. The tall man in the black cape was with him.

When Firingin went to the village courtyard with the elder, he saw the tourist being placed in a dwelling. He wondered why she was being kept, but he wouldn't question his potential benefactor.

Tillya and the other helpers prepared to leave for the Lbaa village. For them, the excitement was over.

"These elders want me to help them," Firingin told Tillya. "Tell the father I will return when I am finished."

Tillya sniffed her contempt. "I am not your messenger," she said. He waved for her to go. He felt too happy to argue.

He ate the evening meal with the elders and sat under a tree while they discussed the clan's options.

Darkness came before they reached consensus.

At sunrise two lmurran would be sent to the road to see if the van was still there. Firingin would go with them. If the tourist people were around, he would explain to them that a mistake had been made and that the woman would be returned.

There had been much debate among the elders about sending the woman on the morning trip with Firingin and the warriors. It was concluded that she was too weak and needed nourishment before she traveled. A woman from the village had tried to feed her, but the thin-skin had eaten nothing except a small amount of honey. In the morning she could be fed blood from a beast or a large portion of goat meat.

After the debate, the elders talked of other matters. Firingin sat under a tree nearby. He felt proud that the elders had confidence in him. It was an unfamiliar feeling. The father only had faith that he could tend the animals—like a child he was trusted to do that.

The air had cooled and Firingin fell asleep.

A nudge awakened him. It was Lominchira, the elder with the cap. "It is time," he said.

It was not morning, but Firingin stretched and followed.

"You must talk to the thin-skin," Lominchira said. "Tell her that we mean no harm and will soon send her back."

They went to the dwelling where the tourist had been placed. The warrior leader sat by its doorway, and his eyes looked worried. Perhaps the elders had reconsidered cursing him over the mistake with the tourist.

Lominchira paid no attention to the warrior. He entered the dwelling without speaking, and Firingin followed. The elder started a fire in the hearth, and shadows moved against the walls. The tourist sat huddled in a corner near the doorway. Her eyes looked bright with fear.

"Speak to her," Lominchira commanded.

Firingin wondered what he could he say? Would the tourist's weak Swahili allow him to convey the elder's meaning?

He greeted her. She had already used the greeting word on the trail.

"Hello, Master," she replied. Her voice was faint.

"There has been a mistake," he said. The phrase was a familiar one from the book of simple Swahili.

He waited. After a moment, she said words that sounded like, "Will you help me?"

He nodded and turned to the elder. "She wants to know if we will help her."

"Tell her yes," the older man said. "That is what we want her to know."

Firingin nodded again and turned back to the woman.

He would make more conversation to be sure he understood her way of speaking.

"What do you want?" he asked.

"Take me back," she answered.

It was what he expected, but he relayed the request to the elder.

The old one nodded. "Tell her we will, tomorrow."

"Tomorrow?" Firingin asked. He did not believe it could be done so soon unless the tourists were still waiting on the road.

"Yes, tomorrow. Tell her!"

"Tomorrow," he said in Swahili.

The tourist smiled a weak smile. The elder smiled and patted Firingin on the back. Firingin and the elder left.

In the light of the following morning, Firingin and the warriors crept along the tribal pathway near the highway to Maralal. It was shortly after sunrise, and thornbushes along the trail glistened where early rays struck the dew. The warriors and Firingin had made good time. They would soon arrive at the site where the previous day's blunder had been committed.

The warriors at Firingin's side were old, nearly as old as the firestick elders who had sent them. But, unlike the ones the day before, these lmurran showed nothing but respect for Firingin. They knew, for they had been told by the elders, that he was the one who could save their clan from police retaliation.

Near the edge of the roadbed, the trio started creeping on their hands and knees. Even before seeing the vehicles and the soldiers, Firingin had heard the sound of the bullhorn's amplified voice.

He and the warriors lay still behind a clump of roadside bushes. He motioned for the other two to wait, and he inched closer for a better look.

The tourist van was gone. In its place were several landrovers and two trucks with canvas coverings. Dozens of soldiers unloaded the trucks. Stacks of boxes and canvas along with machinery and weapons rested around the vehicles.

Firingin listened to the Swahili talk among the green-clad troops. They spoke of an all-out assault that would soon start and of plans to have soldiers go from village to village until they found the woman. The elders and warriors of the village where they found her would be arrested.

Some of the soldiers spoke of shooting Samburus, and others laughed.

Firingin wiggled back to his companions and told them of the danger. The leader of the scouting party directed him to return to the village and to warn the elders. He said that Firingin's young legs could cover the distance quickly and that he and the other warrior would keep watch for a time and then follow.

Firingin left the roadside hiding place through a ravine surrounded by high reeds. He walked in the depression until he came to the first crossing of the path to the village. There he climbed out of the small canyon and started running.

About halfway to the village, he heard the whopping of a helicopter. When he saw it flying low over the bush, he dove into a thornbush cover.

Blood oozed from the punctures in his arms, but he had no time to find mud for a plaster. After the machine screamed past, he left the bushes and raced the rest of the way to the compound.

"Soldiers are coming," he shouted at the group of elders. "They will be here soon."

The elder Lominchira stood and walked toward Firingin. He spoke with a calmness that defied the gravity of the situation. "Did you see the tourist vehicle?"

"No. But it does not matter," Firingin answered. "The soldiers are many, and they will go from village to village until they find the woman. They will arrest all the elders and warriors where they find her."

"There are several villages between here and the road," another elder said. "We must talk of a solution to this problem." The others, even Lominchira, nodded in agreement.

Firingin knew that talk was the way of elders, but he wondered if these men understood the danger.

"Perhaps we should take the tourist to the soldiers," one elder suggested. Another thought, wisely in Firingin's opinion, that they would be shot before they could speak to the soldiers. They discussed hiding her in different places, even disguising her as a Samburu girl. Time did not seem to matter to the old men. They considered all the options, one by one.

While the men talked, Firingin stood at a distance and thought through a solution of his own. He knew the headmaster at the school in Maralal. If he could take the woman to him, the teacher might be able to explain the foolish mistake to the police.

Firingin moved close to Lominchira and told him the idea. The elder listened carefully. His eyes glowed with admiration.

"It would be a day's trip," he said. "The woman cannot travel fast. You will be in danger."

"I am clothed as a child, elder one," Firingin said, "but I have the years of a man. This will be my way of proving my manhood to all Samburus."

"It will indeed," Lominchira replied. He turned to the others and explained Firingin's offer. The others, no doubt seeing how the plan would remove the woman from their village, quickly accepted.

Firingin stood, and Lominchira came and stood before him. "The woman is ready," the elder said. "She ate well this morning. Roast lamb was to her liking."

Firingin clapped a hand over his empty scabbard. He had not retrieved his knife from where it stuck in the snake. "I lack a weapon," he said.

"You shall have mine," Lominchira replied. He reached under his blanket and pulled out the most handsome knife Firingin had ever seen.

Its blade was long and straight as his own had been, but the handle was the tip of a rhinoceros horn. Around the handle's base, above the blade shield, glistened a ring of red jewels, rubies, imbedded in a band of gold.

Lominchira handed the weapon to Firingin. "The handle is to bring fertility," the elder said. "But I am too old for such things."

Firingin turned the knife over in his hands and felt tears come. Ashamed, he looked at the sky.

"Now, go to the tourist," Lominchira said. "When you have safely returned her, come back to me. A man with such a knife as yours should not live as a herdsboy."

10

Leslie sat inside the hut's doorway and closed her eyes. She desperately needed sleep, but a noisy pair of boubou birds kept her awake. She knew what they were because Calvin, an expert on African birds, had pointed them out at the camp in the Mara.

Her guard was no longer at his post, but she could see him moping under a tree across the courtyard.

Through her night of fitful sleep, she had awakened numerous times and had pondered the motives of the Samburu. If they had wanted her for entertainment, they wouldn't have kept her shut up like she was. Besides, the man in black had stated that it was a mistake. But why on earth had they brought her here? How could they have marched her all those miles without knowing what they were doing?

Her stomach gurgled. The lamb meat the woman had served her had been edible enough, but it had contained a lifetime supply of cholesterol and just plain grease.

The boubous finally flew. Leslie dozed intermittently until someone entered the hovel. She rubbed her eyes and recognized the intruder as the tall man.

"Hello," she said.

He motioned for her to stand.

The man's eyes sparkled with excitement. Something must have happened to him since last night. He had taken on an attitude of complete confidence—almost as if he were now in charge. She couldn't believe how much his situation had improved since yesterday. Then he was, apparently, a prisoner, submissively taking orders, and today he acted like a chief.

Responding to his forceful manner, she stood without thinking and banged her head into the hovel's roof.

"I am sorry," he said.

After a moment, he motioned her toward the doorway.

"Come," he said. His Swahili sounded gentle, almost reassuring.

"Where do I go?" she said. She was able to use one of the few sentences from the native language that she knew.

He pointed to one of the openings in the barricade.

"Mistress go back now."

She walked with him toward the portal and noticed people from the village watching. They weren't crowding, as they had yesterday. They stood silently at a distance.

An impulse struck her, and she waved. She couldn't explain it. Somehow she felt sad about leaving them. In spite of the discomfort she had endured, she sensed that the Samburus were a friendly people. She wished, in a way, she could have stayed a few days longer. If she could have gotten out of that hovel, she might have enjoyed the experience.

Outside the barricade, the tall man pointed toward a

pathway under the trees. She hesitated. It wasn't the route to the road. At least she didn't think it was.

"Is this the way?" she asked. Another sentence!

She knew more than she'd thought. He nodded and with a firm hand, directed her toward the growth-covered trail.

"There is no problem," he said.

She smiled. His words were the title of a Swahili song she had sung with her fellow tourists. She started humming the refrain, and the tall man smiled. He had a nice smile.

They passed through an area canopied by large trees and then to a dry streambed that was surrounded by stands of reeds. In the sandy waterway, the tall man walked fast. She lagged behind, and he started dragging her by the hand.

She jerked away. "No!" she said.

He smiled again. "Please," he said. "We must hurry."

She wondered about his urgency. Perhaps it was because her return had already been scheduled. She would try to keep up. Maybe she would soon be telling these adventures to Mary and the others. Maybe Johanna could even explain what had happened to her and possibly what had produced the miraculous change in the tall man.

Leslie had to admit that she liked the tall man. He sometimes seemed fierce—like the way he was with the boy by the road—but his voice was gentle when he spoke to Leslie. She decided to asked him his name.

"Firingin," he answered, without breaking stride.

"Firingin," she repeated. "And my name is Leslie."

He nodded.

They continued in silence.

Suddenly he stopped and held up his hand. A short distance ahead, the brooding face and curved-down horns of an African buffalo peered from behind the reeds.

Leslie gasped. She'd been told by someone in the tour group that African buffaloes were the most dangerous animals in Kenya.

She drew back. Firingin shook his head at her. It was true,

she shouldn't show fear. She inched behind him and stood as still as possible. The air filled with small noises—insects, the rustling of leaves and even her own breathing. Suddenly the animal bolted into the brush. A thunder of hooves from the other side of the reeds revealed the herd that had lurked behind him.

"That was a close call," she said. Firingin looked puzzled. He evidently didn't understand any English.

He smiled and pointed in the direction they'd been traveling. Without further discussion, they resumed their obsessive race against time.

After they'd traveled another mile or so, an open area appeared at the end of the dry streambed. Firingin signaled another halt.

"Wait," he said, and went alone to a place where the vegetation parted.

Leslie sat down and rubbed her feet while she watched him crouch behind a clump of reeds near the opening. After several minutes, he came back and without explanation drew his knife. He inspected it, almost reverently, she thought.

She quickly put on her shoes and stood up. She'd trusted him so far, she'd actually had no choice, but now he was acting scary. She knew practically nothing about African tribes and their traditions. Maybe the Samburus had captured her in order to fulfill some ritualistic requirement. Maybe she was now going to be...she wouldn't even think it.

She closed her eyes and waited. From this place, she wouldn't know which way to run.

Presently she heard chopping sounds. She looked and saw Firingin, without his cape on, cutting reeds from a nearby stand.

She felt foolish when she saw him using the knife as a machete, but who would have expected it. He'd been hurrying like mad since they left, so why would anyone think he had the time to harvest vegetation.

She sat down again to watch. As Firingin worked, the

muscles of his body rolled and his skin glistened with perspiration. She felt her pulse quicken.

Frowning, she cautioned herself. This was no time for erotic fantasies.

Firingin stacked the stalks under a nearby tree. He seemed to be building something—perhaps a signal fire.

She'd heard helicopters flying in the distance.

She kept watching as he crawled in and out of an opening he'd made at the base of the stack. After a time, he stood back and inspected his work.

"Please," he said, motioning her toward the opening.

His behavior continually puzzled her. "I do not understand," she said.

"There is no problem," he replied.

She crawled inside, and he followed her. A fresh smell engulfed them. It was a scent so strong that it even overpowered Firingin's sour milk odor. She sat on the dirt floor and looked around. Firingin had stripped most of the leaves from the stalks, but the sloping walls still hung with green. A muted light came through the layers of vegetation, and its glow reminded Leslie of an undersea grotto.

Firingin took a position near the doorway. He grinned at her, and she wondered why. Why did he look so pleased with himself?

Her imagination took off again. Maybe he was still preparing her for a tribal ceremony. Such ritualistic responsibility would certainly be an explanation for his sudden change into a man with a mission.

She edged away from him, and her back touched the cool vegetation of the wall. She let out a yelp.

Everything now frightened her.

She moved a few inches toward the center of the enclosure. She was caught between her fear of things that could be crawling through the leafy walls and dread of what might be in the mind of the determined man at her side.

She glared at him. "Take me back. Now!" Without thinking, she'd spoken in English, and he looked puzzled.

"Please," he said. "There is no problem."

She stammered, trying to put her meaning in Swahili.

A look of concern grew in his eyes. He seemed like he wanted to help but didn't know how.

She sat staring at him. It was true. He wasn't acting like a cruel man. If he'd been meaning to hurt her, he'd had plenty of chances. And if native Africans sacrificed tourist women, it would have been news all over the world.

She smiled at him. Perhaps, like he'd said, his mission was to return her. But, she wondered, why didn't he just do it?

The afternoon wore on, and the moisture and heat inside the enclosure increased to steambath proportions.

Except for brief moments when Firingin pushed a branch from the doorway to look outside, there was no movement of air inside their green dwelling.

Insects began crawling out of the wall, and Leslie cringed when she saw them. Africa was full of nasty bugs—many were deadly.

Firingin hacked several of the intruders into pieces.

"Centipedes," he said. The Swahili word was one of the few that she knew outside of greetings and phases used by tourists. She wished she knew more things to say. It was maddening to just sit and not be able to communicate with him.

She could say "Asante sana." And each time he killed one of the insects, she thanked him. He grinned.

Maybe her words sounded funny.

He must have decided that she needed help. He started pointing at things and saying words in Swahili.

Occasionally she heard one that she recognized, but usually he spoke too fast.

To pass the time, she recited all the Swahili she knew. He grinned with each of her attempts. Several times he tried to correct her. The words sounded completely different when he said them.

It didn't take long for her to go through her entire vocabulary. It became oppressively hot, and even language lessons took too much effort. Leslie and Firingin sat in silence. He kept looking outside, probably to be sure no animal was sneaking up on them. Or perhaps he expected some humans to be coming for her.

Night came, and the celestial furnace that had driven heat through the layers of reeds went over the horizon. The sweatbox began to cool.

A hyrax screamed in a tree above the dwelling, and Leslie jumped at the sound. Calvin had said that the tree hyrax had the worst animal cry in all of Africa. Everyone in the tour group had talked about the fierce screams in the night.

When Leslie jumped, her shoulder bumped into Firingin. In the darkness, it felt good to touch him. There was a feeling of security from the physical contact.

She decided to stay close to him.

After a time, he moved to take one of his looks outside, and he remained near the doorway. She edged toward him, but he moved away.

Maybe, like all the other men in her life, Firingin had been repelled by her presence.

She sat brooding in the darkness until she felt the grasp of his hand on her arm.

"Come," he said. "It is time."

He spoke slowly, so she understood his words. But how did he know what time it was?

"Go back now," he added.

Feeling a surge of excitement, she followed him to the doorway. Maybe she would emerge from the grotto to an assembled welcoming committee from the tour group. Like people at a surprise birthday celebration, they could have been gathering in silence.

Outside there was nothing. Only the darkness met her.

Firingin took her hand and led her to the opening he had inspected that morning. Beyond the reeds, they picked up a trail that seemed to lead into a wide savanna. More like the area where the van had stalled, this region was covered with high bushes and stretches of dull grass.

Again, Firingin wanted to hurry, and Leslie had trouble keeping up. Unused to walking so much, her feet had grown painfully sore. Eventually she had to stop.

She sat down in the middle of the path and rubbed her arches and ankles.

Firingin seemed angry and tried to pull her up.

"Please, come," he said.

She shook her head. "No! I can't. My feet hurt."

Without speaking again, he leaned across and placed her arms around his neck. He stood and boosted her onto his back.

Hefting her once, as if she were a child, he elevated her to his shoulders. Then he resumed his hurried gait.

She rode with her legs astride his neck, his head protruding from between her thighs. Her shorts pulled up tight, and she felt uncomfortable at first. She shifted positions, and soon the rhythm of his body helped her to relax. Before long, she began to enjoy her lofty position and the view it gave her.

The magic of the scene, grass looking almost velvet under the light of the stars, and the feeling of Firingin's strong shoulders beneath her had an unsettling effect. She suddenly found herself becoming sexually aroused. She felt embarrassed and cleared her throat.

"Is mistress all right?" Firingin asked.

"Yes!" she said. She hoped her answer hadn't sounded too desperate.

Thankfully, his question had helped break the spell.

To keep it broken, she concentrated on the distant view.

Lights of automobile traffic traced a road across a range of low hills near the horizon. Several times she saw the red flasher of an emergency vehicle. Maybe people were actually out looking for her.

Ahead she noticed a glow in the sky. It looked like the lights of a town. She wondered if it was the game sanctuary that Sammy had been trying to reach.

Maybe it was also Firingin's destination. She tapped the top of his head and pointed toward the glow. "Town?" she asked.

He nodded. "Maralal."

After a time, he started to sing a low and haunting melody. She had more questions but didn't want to interrupt.

Completely calm now, she looked up at the canopy of stars—billions and billions as Carl Sagan would say.

She marveled at their beauty. Across the darkness, the milky way was a swath of brilliant gold.

Firingin descended a steep incline, and they came to a forested area. When the trail leveled, he stopped.

The glow in the sky was all around. They were close to Maralal.

Firingin lowered her to the ground and pointed to a clump of thornbushes.

"Go, please," he whispered. He gently pushed her toward a barely visible opening.

She hated crawling into brushy places in the dark, but she'd given up resisting his commands. With him close behind, she obediently crawled through.

On the other side, a rocky slope descended toward a small canyon. A pair of warthogs scampered away from the thornbushes. They startled her, and she fell back into Firingin.

"Pigs," he said and laughed. It was the first time she'd seen him laugh. So serious most of the time, his face suddenly looked boyish. When she looked back at the animals, only the antennae of their tails revealed their frantic zigzags through the grass.

Firingin moved in front and took her hand in his.

They soon entered the canyon and, following the trail it provided, approached the town.

Leslie checked her watch. It was almost midnight.

She wondered who he would deliver her to at that hour. Yet sounds of vehicles and even voices in the distance made it seem possible that many residents were still awake.

Firingin didn't seem to notice the noises. He led her under a bridge and across a field toward a row of small, dilapidated houses. He stopped by a hedgerow and took off his cape. When he started to wrap it over Leslie's head, she pushed him away.

"No!" she said.

Over the past day she had gotten somewhat accustomed to the smell of his body, but she wouldn't want to risk breathing through a piece of his clothing.

"Please, Leslie," he said. It was the first time he had used her name. From him, it sounded strange—the "s" hissy, like an evangelist saying "Jesus."

She smiled. At least he cared enough to remember her name.

He handed the cape back to her. "Please help me," he said. The pleading look in his eyes melted her resolve. Maybe she could hold her breath for a while.

"How long will it take?" she asked.

"Not long."

A sadness engulfed her. Then it would soon be over, and she'd be leaving him. She would miss this tall native. He'd been as gentle and patient as any man she had ever known. In a short span of time she had grown to feel real affection for him. Now she'd have to forget him and return to the likes of Owen Polier.

She breathed a sigh and nearly choked on the smell of the cape. She shook her head. She couldn't get sentimental at this point—not over a man who, except for remembering her name one time, had shown nothing but an attitude of dutiful attendance.

11

Firingin led the tourist through the predawn darkness. They had entered Maralal, but he would stay away from the streets. Soldiers on the road would also be in Maralal.

Behind fences and shrubbery, he crept with the woman named Leslie. He said nothing, leading her by the hand until they reached the dwelling of his mother's sister.

By a dark clump of oleanders, he stopped. "Wait here," he said and went alone to the door.

The tourist coughed under the cloak. She had weak breathing, but he could not remove the cover from her. The light color of her hair could be easily seen.

The sister would give them shelter. The sister had never lived among the Samburu, and she had always been kind to

Firingin. She had come south when Firingin's mother came to marry the father and had never gone back to Rendille country. She lived by herself and made strings of beads and jewelry that she sold in the Maralal market. During the seasons, over four years when Firingin had attended the government school, he had stayed with her.

He rattled the door panel of her dwelling. There was no answer, but he knew she would be home. The sister never traveled. He shook the panel again.

"Who is it?" The sister's voice had become cracked from shouting at the market.

"It is Firingin," he answered, "your nephew from the Lbaa clan." If this had been a Samburu village, such formality would have been insulting to the dwelling's owner but not in Maralal.

The door opened and the sister rubbed her eyes.

"Firingin!" she said. She was wrapped in a blanket. She must have been sleeping.

"I'm glad to see you, but why are you here?" she added.

He pointed to the tourist standing in the shadows.

"I need the shelter of your dwelling for this woman."

The sister pushed the panel wide open and stepped outside. "Woman?" she said. The sister seemed to be slow waking up. "Why have you brought a woman to me? And why is her face covered?"

"We must come inside," Firingin said. "Then I will explain."

She motioned for them to enter, and he led the tourist from her hiding place.

The tourist uncovered her head, and the sister stared at her. "She has light hair. Who is she?"

"A thin-skin sought by the police," he replied.

The sister pulled her door panel closed. "The police!" she said. "Yes, I saw them today in the market. There were many, and they spoke of a tourist woman who'd been kidnapped by the Samburu. Did you take her?"

Firingin shook his head. "It was a mistake made by a group

of young warriors. But I am returning her."

The sister walked around the woman, holding a candle high to spread its light. She stared at Firingin. "Why do you want her in my house?"

"She will not be here long," he said. "I will go to the headmaster at the school in the morning. He will take her to the police."

"You must be careful. I saw patrols on the streets when I came home from my stall. Some talked of shooting Samburus."

"The school is not far. I will go alone and will bring the headmaster here."

"You must not lead the police to my house!"

"I will go before sunrise and stay hidden."

"This woman looks frail," the sister said. "Does she need food?"

"We have not eaten since morning. The tourist does not enjoy food. You can use your English and ask if she will eat."

The sister spoke to the tourist with drifty-sounding words. Firingin could not understand what she said, but the tourist smiled and talked rapidly.

"I will make a fire," the sister said. "She says she is hungry. These white ones are like sheep. They cannot go long without food. I have fresh produce from yesterday's market. She says she will eat vegetables."

He nodded.

The tourist and the sister talked while the sister cooked. They said many things. Sometimes the sister repeated what they said for Firingin.

"She doesn't know what happened to her," the sister said. "Why was she taken? I don't know the answer. What mistake was made?"

Firingin explained, as best he could, the foolishness of the warriors.

The sister and the woman talked more. "She asks who killed the snake. Was it you?"

He nodded. "The warriors took me prisoner before I could

retrieve my knife. An elder of the primitive clan gave me this." He showed the jeweled weapon to the sister.

Her eyes glistened. "Why it must be worth a thousand shillings," she said. "That's a rhino horn, you know."

He nodded again. "And he promised to help me regain my status if I safely return this woman."

The sister smiled. "Now I see why you take such risks."

She turned back to the tourist and talked more English. The sister pointed at Firingin, and the tourist smiled and reached to shake his hand. He felt embarrassed.

They ate. When they had finished, the tourist talked many words to the sister. The sister brought her a bowl of water, and the woman did something Firingin had never seen before. She removed pieces of her eyes and washed them in the water.

"What does she do?" he asked.

"She says they are contacts. She cleans them for better seeing."

He felt his own eyes. No seeing-pieces came loose.

He picked up the bowl and looked at the magic eye-circles under the water. When he looked up, he saw the tourist grinning at him.

The sister piled blankets and robes near the back wall. "You have a big day tomorrow and so do I," she said. "We must sleep."

The cooking fire burned to coals. The sister's snores floated from her bedroom, and Firingin could not sleep. He looked at the plywood ceiling and thought of his return to status. He would probably be made a warrior. He smiled. The father could not punish a warrior.

Firingin looked at the tourist. Her body curled on the edge of the bedding. She had fallen asleep with her face on the dirt of the floor. The tourist was thin, but her skin was smooth. With her eyes closed, dark lashes were on her cheeks.

He wondered what kind of a life she came from. She had magic circles for seeing, but she seemed helpless and afraid.

Had her world not prepared her for dangers?

His eyes scanned the tourist's curled up form. He wondered what she looked like under her clothes and what it would be like to have sex with her. He had enjoyed sex often with the uncircumcised girls of the clan. He'd entered Tillya, the most playful Lbaa girl, numerous times before she had gone through the Lmugit rites. It would be permissible for him to have sex with this tourist. All thin-skin women were uncircumcised.

Sex with Leslie would be permitted by the Samburu, but he would not attempt to enter her. He'd heard from other boys at the school how thin-skin women fear sex.

He would not frighten this Leslie, the one he'd promised to return safely.

He gazed at the shadows in the room. The sister's dwelling, windowless as a Samburu lodge, was familiar to him. Her walls hung with objects that she owned. Boxes of shells and beads for her jewelry making were stacked on the floor. He regarded the place near the hearth where he'd sat in the past for meals. The sister had many pots and dishes. Such things must be familiar to the tourist.

The fire in the hearth burned out. The sister stopped snoring, and darkness finally brought sleep to Firingin.

In the misty light of early morning, the familiar structures of the Maralal School loomed ahead of Firingin. He darted across the yard to the small equipment shed that stood behind the main building. It had never been locked, and he would hide there until the teachers arrived.

He had seen the headmaster only once since he was a student, but he still considered the man to be his friend. Though a Nandi, the headmaster was wise and knew the ways of the Samburu. He would comprehend that foolish warriors sometimes make mistakes. His respectability would allow him to explain that to the police.

The sun rose to more than two hands above the horizon. Firingin heard no voices, so he opened the shed's door a small crack. All seemed quiet.

He crept to one of the windows in the main building.

Inside, no electric bulbs were lit and no people were visible. Cautiously, he went to a side door and shook the handle. No one answered.

He checked the sun again. It was well past the normal starting hour for classes. He returned to the shed. While he pondered the situation, he remembered. Unlike the Samburus, who did things by the daily needs of the beasts or by tradition, the people who ran the school made schedules by a paper calendar. The school must be closed on this day.

It was mid-morning, and without the headmaster at his side, Firingin feared leading the police to the sister's dwelling. It would also be risky to stay through the long day at the school.

He checked outside to be sure that no one was on the grounds, and he left the shed.

He ran to the ditch behind the school. To avoid detection, he would follow it to the drainage canal that passed close to the sister's home.

He had gone only a short distance along the ditch when he heard the onrushing sound of a helicopter. For the second time in two days, he dove for cover.

The depression where he hid was deep, but still he forced himself to lay as still as a rock under a tangle of tamarisk. When the chopping sound faded, he ran to the drainage canal and then to the orchard behind the sister's dwelling.

From hedge to hedge and tree to tree, he dashed across the field. He checked to be sure he hadn't been followed. Then he raced to the door.

"Where is the schoolmaster?" the sister asked when he came inside.

"No one is at the school. I could not wait longer."

The sister looked disappointed.

"What will you do now?"

He didn't know.

The sister wrung her hands. She seemed afraid.

"Today I will ask at the market," she said. "If the school is closed, someone should know."

Firingin gazed at the tourist. She was still asleep.

He tried to think of options. If the school was closed, it could be days before the headmaster returned. It would be too much danger for the sister if he and the woman waited in her dwelling. He could not return with the tourist to the primitive clan's village. Also, he could not take her to the Lbaa village. The father would be angry and might do harm to the tourist.

"Did you hear the flying machine?" the sister asked.

Firingin nodded. "I dove under bushes, and it flew away. I was not seen."

The sister made a weak smile.

The tourist must have heard them talking. She moved in the bedding and moaned.

"She's been doing that," the sister said. "She sat up one time and shivered. I wonder if she's sick."

"Do you have herbs for her?"

"I have herbs, but I must know what is wrong before I use them."

The sister handed Firingin a bowl of millet and a cup of tea. "Here, eat," she said. "I must go now to the market. When the woman wakes, feed her some honey."

The sister gathered her leather bags and started toward the door.

"We should not stay," Firingin said.

"If the woman is sick, she cannot travel," the sister replied. She left before he could argue against her wisdom.

Firingin went to the fireplace and set the teapot over the flames.

Another helicopter flew over. Its roar woke the tourist, and she came to the hearth. He gave her the honey, but she seemed dreamy and didn't eat.

She murmured something that he didn't understand.

She made a circle with her hand and pointed up. He nodded.

She sipped at her tea.
The tourist's face looked red. Maybe it was her redness that made her shiver. He'd known that thin-skins get sick from the sun. It was the reason he'd built the reed shelter for yesterday's wait. Perhaps its protection had been weak.
She curled her body beside the fireplace.
"Mistress?" she asked in Swahili. "Is the mistress home?"
"No," he answered.
The tourist looked toward the door. "When will we go?" she asked.
"Soon," he said. He said soon, but he did not know when. "Maybe tonight," he added.
The woman tasted the honey. She smiled.
"Thank you much," she said. "Tastes good."
"Good for you," he said. She nodded and sat up for more tea. She must have been cold. She sat close to him and pulled a blanket over their shoulders.
He felt the warmth of her skin and wondered again how it would be to enter her. He sat still and waited for the feeling to leave.
She fell asleep, and he watched her.
When the sister came home, she had herb leaves and potions. "I had a good day," she said. "So I purchased a variety of medicines and also a good piece of meat." She placed a package of red beef on the cooking slab.
"Brisket of ox," she said and fanned the coals of the fire to flames.
She pointed at the sleeping form of the tourist.
"How is she?"
"Her skin is red," he answered. "I think she is sick from the sun."
The sister nodded and pounded the meat.
"Did you hear any talk about the school?" he asked.
"I asked the woman in the stall next to mine. She said children on her street have been home for a week. She hopes they will go back soon."

"Did you see any police?"

"All day long they were in the market. Since the Samburus are staying away from town, police and soldiers are my main customers. They buy my beads for their girlfriends."

"What did they say?"

The sister shook her head. "Samburu villages all the way to Losiolo have been searched. One soldier told of screaming and crying from the people when roofs were ripped from dwellings and the herds were stampeded."

Firingin felt sadness. The father would surely place a curse on him for being away at such a time.

"I will take the tourist to the soldiers," he said. "My status will not be restored after such devastation."

"The woman is still weak," the sister said. "Besides, the soldiers might shoot you. They talk of shooting Samburus in the town."

"The soldiers brag. They would not shoot if the woman was with me."

"They might shoot because she was with you," the sister said. "Stay a few days," she added. "The teachers may come back. They're usually not gone longer than a week. You should know that."

He nodded. "I will try once again tomorrow. If the headmaster is not there, I will take the woman to the police."

"Just don't bring the police back here," the sister said.

The tourist must have smelled the food. She came from the back of the room and sat between Firingin and the sister. The sister talked to her.

"I told the woman about the police," the sister said. "She says you must not risk getting killed."

"After tomorrow, I may not have a choice."

Firingin went to the blankets. The woman and sister talked until late. When the woman came to the blankets, she removed her clothes before she laid down.

Later, he felt her come to him, and the excitement grew in his body.

12

When Leslie awoke, she had the most serene feeling she had ever known. She'd experienced orgasms before, private ones, but never like last night. With Firingin inside her, they had just kept coming. Without looking, she reached for him. He wasn't there!

She felt a twinge of panic. What if he had left, disappointed?

She rolled over and looked at the place where he'd been. How could he be disappointed when it had been so wonderful?

She pinched herself to be sure she wasn't dreaming. It seemed unbelievable that she, a woman who had scarcely talked to a man, could have had sex with a native African.

It was even more unbelievable that she had initiated it herself.

At first, it had been innocent enough. Her clothes had smelled bad, so she'd decided to take them off before lying down.

Firingin had already been on the bedding, but not asleep. As usual, he'd seemed aloof. She'd moved toward him, maybe just to see how he would react. Their bodies had touched, and she'd felt his penis, hard and warm, against her side. After that, passion had simply taken over.

She felt a moment's guilt. Leslie Halstrom was definitely not the kind of woman who did such things. It could have been the influence of the native culture—everybody running around nearly naked. Or it could have been riding astride his neck under the stars. Away from the cow dung and the rancid grease of the Samburu village, even Firingin's smell had begun to arouse her.

Leslie looked around the room. His aunt's house was a shack with a dirt floor, but a person could at least stand upright. She wondered if she could accept living in a place like this.

Firingin's aunt was a likable person. Maikonila was the woman's name, and she seemed to love talking with her funny-sounding English. The first night, she'd told Leslie that she was a sister of Firingin's mother. The two women had grown up in a clan that wasn't Samburu—Rendille she'd called it. Leslie remembered that Sammy had talked about Rendille camel drivers who lived in the North. Maikonila had come to this place when Firingin's mother came to be married. Maikonila had never married.

She'd told Leslie that Firingin had never seen his mother's people. Maikonila said she had kept in touch with them and had sent messages about Firingin when he'd lived with her as a student. The fact that Firingin had lived with his aunt as a child impressed Leslie. It was a similarity to Leslie's own childhood that she couldn't ignore.

Maikonila had told Leslie many things about Firingin. He was the one who had saved Leslie from the snake, and now he was risking his life to take her back to the tour group.

She wondered why. Was he simply the heroic type, or did

Firingin really care for her? Until last night, she'd never guessed he even saw her as a woman.

She shrugged. She couldn't let herself get carried away. She would soon be leaving. She'd have memories of her brave African and their wonderful night of love but that would be all.

A sound came from Maikonila's room. Leslie pulled a blanket over herself.

Firingin's aunt emerged from behind the curtain.

Tall and statuesque, maybe forty years of age, Maikonila was a striking woman. She seemed as self-assured as any female school principal Leslie had ever known. Leslie liked Maikonila and sensed that her feelings of friendship were returned.

"Why he's gone to the school," Maikonila said when Leslie asked about Firingin. "He wants to talk to the headmaster. Didn't I tell you?"

"I thought you said we were here so Firingin could take me back to my tour group. What's he doing with a schoolmaster?"

"Firingin needs that man's help to return you."

Leslie tried to comprehend the meaning of her answer.

"But why doesn't he just take me to the police?" she said. "Isn't that what you said would happen?"

"Firingin cannot take you to the police. He is Samburu. The police would arrest him. They might even shoot him."

Leslie frowned. Maikonila had said something last night about shooting, but Leslie hadn't thought she was serious. "That's awful!"

"I told Firingin not to go to the police."

"And he's using this headmaster as some kind of a mediator?"

"That word I do not know. All I can tell you is Firingin wants the headmaster to take you to the police and explain the warriors' mistake. It would have been done by now if yesterday the school had not been closed."

Leslie touched the place on the blankets where he had been. "I'm glad it was," she said.

Maikonila looked at her curiously. "I don't understand

your words," she said. "Are you happy to still be here?"

Leslie shook her head. "No, it's not that," she said. "I'm just glad he's OK."

Maikonila shrugged. "You must eat."

Leslie nodded. She wrapped the blanket around her shoulders and stood up.

Maikonila handed her a bowl of cereal stirred up in honey. "How do you feel this morning?" she asked.

The question took Leslie aback. She wondered if Maikonila had heard them in the night. She smiled, trying to look nonchalant.

"Yesterday you seemed sick," Maikonila added.

"Oh, I was exhausted, but now I'm fine."

Maikonila nodded. She regarded the windup clock on the kitchen shelf. "Firingin has been gone for nearly three hours," she said. "The headmaster must be there."

Leslie checked her watch. It didn't show the same time as the clock, but both read after 10:30—later than any school's start time.

"Soon they will come for you," Maikonila said.

Leslie tried to look pleased, but she felt sad. It had hit her that she'd never again be with him.

"I must go now," Maikonila said. She picked up a handful of leather bags. "I sold everything I had yesterday. So many soldiers in town."

"Here because of me?" Leslie said.

Maikonila nodded. "They search for you in the Samburu villages. They tell of destroying the dwellings and running off the animals."

"How ghastly!"

"The reprisals could go on for weeks if the mistake is not explained to the police. The Kenyan's do not want tribal people interfering with the tourists."

"And that's why Firingin needs the schoolmaster?"

"Yes. He must have a respected man to make the explanation."

"Firingin must be a great chief to have such a responsibility."

Maikonila laughed. "Firingin?" she said. "He is no chief. He has no status at all among the Samburu. They do not even consider him a man."

Leslie shook her head. Of all people, how could Firingin not be considered a man?

"I don't understand," she said.

Maikonila waved her hands. "I haven't time to explain." She walked to the door. "I won't be back until evening, so I won't see you again." She extended a hand to Leslie. "I'll say good-bye."

"Oh, yes. Good-bye and thanks for everything."

"Stay inside until Firingin comes. I don't want the police chasing you back to my house."

Maikonila left, and Leslie went to the blankets. She looked at the place where she and Firingin had made love.

A layer of tears rose in her eyes.

13

Loud voices outside the shed woke Firingin from a fitful and sweaty sleep. He rubbed his eyes and peered through a crack in the wall. He saw a line of people standing on the opposite side of the courtyard. He recognized it as the afternoon queue for the school's medical clinic.

He must have been sleeping for hours. In the morning, when he'd arrived, all had been quiet, like the day before. He'd considered leaving to return to the woman, but decided to stay when he remembered that the headmaster sometimes came late to his office on days when the school was closed. It must have been the heat inside the shed that had brought the sleep.

The people in the line would recognize him as a Samburu, so he would wait until they left. He leaned his back against a beam inside the wall and thought of the woman.

Such moaning and writhing during sex he had never known. He wondered if it was the way of the thin-skins to curse their women with such ghosts of pleasure. When her gyrations had first started, his surprise had made him back away, but she had pulled him back into her. It could have been the strange face-to-face position that caused her unusual reactions. If they had sex again, he would make her accept entry from behind. The natural way would be better, and he could calm her by holding her breasts.

Violent as the sex had been with the thin-skin woman, he'd enjoyed it even more than with Tillya.

Before he took the woman to the police, he would enter her another time. It had not made her angry. Besides, his return to status was already lost.

Shouts came from outside. Firingin placed his eye to the peephole. The people were scattering from the line. He couldn't see why until a pair of soldiers entered his field of view. His pulse quickened. The soldiers approached the clinic and waved their automatic rifles at the people. The green-uniformed men climbed the stairs to the porch of the medical building. One kicked aside an old man who lingered by the doorway, and they went inside.

Firingin thought of taking a chance on leaving, but the patients quickly returned to the line. They would have shouted to the soldiers if they saw him. He continued to watch.

He wondered why the soldiers were there. Maybe the woman, Leslie, had become impatient, waiting alone in the sister's dwelling. She might have gone to the police by herself and sent them to the school.

The doctors would know nothing of him, but the soldiers might search the clinic and the other buildings.

Soon it would be dark, and he would leave.

Another commotion sent the people scurrying from the line. One of the soldiers had come out of the building.

He seemed to be questioning the patients. Each one's head

shook after he spoke. The soldier looked disgusted.

When he reached the end of the line, he shouldered his weapon and walked away.

The people grew quiet. No more patients were served, and one by one they left. The other soldier stayed inside the clinic, and Firingin thought again of making his escape. He could not see any people but knew that some might remain beyond his view. He would wait for the darkness.

He thought again of the woman. He hoped he was wrong about her going to the police. He wanted her to be at the sister's dwelling when he got there. He wanted to have sex with the woman and to see the glow in her eyes.

Voices came from the direction of the medical clinic. The soldier had come out on the porch with a doctor. The soldier pointed to the main building of the school. The doctor waved his hand and returned to his clinic. The soldier started across the courtyard.

The shadows, long in the late afternoon light, made the soldier seem giant-sized as he walked. It was nearly dark, but it was too late for Firingin's escape.

The soldier was coming to the shed!

Firingin looked around the room for a place to hide. It was a small area, cluttered with tools and cartons of cleaning materials. In the back, near a stack of brooms and rakes, sat a large drum. Waist high to a man, the drum would provide cover if Firingin crouched low.

After hours in the shed's dim interior, his eyes had adapted. He had no trouble moving quickly to the spot between the drum and the back wall.

He waited for what seemed a lifetime. He tried to keep quiet, but the sounds of his body pounded in his ears. If the soldier heard the sounds, he would come directly to the drum. Firingin tried to hold his breath.

The gravel crunched outside, and Firingin unsheathed his knife. He chanced a short intake of air.

A metallic click! The soldier had prepared his weapon.

The bottom of the door panel scraped against the dirt. Firingin's body thundered in his ears. The light had faded outside, and only a glow from the opening spread to the interior.

Firingin had to breathe. It came as a cough!

The soldier moved swiftly. A glint of light traced the path of his rifle to the back wall.

In a frantic effort, Firingin kicked at the stack of brooms. They clattered to the floor, and flames shot from the soldier's weapon. The bullets turned wood and plastic into powder as they sprayed behind the drum. But Firingin was no longer there.

With a lightning twist, he had slipped between the drum and the opposite wall. From behind the soldier, the blade of the jeweled knife flashed. It drove deep into the green-covered back, passing through heart-muscle on its way to a dull scrape against bone.

The soldier slumped dead before the rifle's echo had faded, and Firingin was gone.

"What happened?" the sister asked when he entered her dwelling. "You look like you've seen a ghost."

He breathed hard and didn't answer. His eyes searched for the woman.

She was sitting on the blankets at the back of the room. He looked back to the sister.

"I have killed a soldier," he said. "The woman and I must leave."

The sister said nothing. Her eyes grew large with fear.

"It is not what I wanted," he added, "but he would have killed me."

The sister stared at him for a moment. "Where will you go?"

"I do not know. But I must go. I will bring danger to your dwelling if I stay."

The sister nodded. "Yes, it will not be safe," she said. "They will soon search from house to house."

"I don't believe anyone saw me," he said. He had left so quickly that even the porch light of the clinic had not come on until he was in the bushes.

He thought about places to hide with the woman. "We will have to go to the hills," he said, more to himself than the sister. "There is a cave, one I know from my school days."

"But you cannot stay in a cave with the woman," the sister said. "She will grow restless. She will want to return to her people."

Firingin looked at the tourist woman. She wore a bright-colored wrap, one of the sister's, and her hair was wet as if she'd been swimming.

"Why is she wet?" he asked.

"She wanted to bathe. I gave her soap and a pail of water."

"She does not like smells," he said. "Her own must also offend her."

The woman came from the back of the room and spoke to the sister. The sister talked to her.

"I told her what has happened," the sister told him.

"Tell her to make ready to leave," he said.

"But what will you do with her?"

"In the early morning I will leave her at the school. The soldiers will find her."

"Don't take her to the school, Firingin," the sister said. "The police will be waiting. They will capture you and then come here."

"I will go in the darkness. They will not see me. Besides, I cannot travel far with the woman. She does not walk fast."

"Leave her on a street in Maralal," the sister said. "Then you can go alone to the North to Parsaloi. It is a place where camel caravans stop. You can join one that will take you to the land of the Rendilles. My father, Jeiso Hedaidile, also your grandfather, will give you shelter."

"I will not leave the woman on a street," he said. "The police are crazy. They could shoot her in the town."

"They could also shoot her at the school," the sister said.

"I will not leave her on the streets of Maralal," he shouted.

The sister started to weep. "You must," she said. "You bring danger to yourself if you don't."

"I bring danger to her if I do," he yelled.

The tourist looked angry at him and hugged the sister. The tourist woman did not understand.

He grew impatient with the sister's meddling words.

"Tell the woman to make ready," he said.

"This is lunacy," she said. She rubbed the tears from her eyes and talked to the tourist. The woman listened. She seem to grow fearful and talked loud to the sister.

"She says she will not go to a cave."

"She has no choice," he said. "Tell her."

After the sister spoke, the woman looked sad and went to the back of the room.

"I must pack some blankets, food, and cooking wares," the sister said.

"We do not have time," he replied.

"She will grow weak and die if she is forced to eat and drink as a Samburu. You must carry supplies."

He did not understand why the sister suddenly worried about the tourist's health.

"I cannot carry bundles of things," he replied. "I may have to carry the woman."

The tourist continued to look fearful. Her eyes glowed with resentment, and he grew anxious to leave.

If the tourist woman fought him, he would have to tie her. He did not want to tie her.

The sister handed him one of the bundles and also a tablet of paper with a pencil. "You will have to talk to this woman," she said. "If she doesn't understand, draw pictures for your words."

He took the tablet, and the sister took the other bundle to the tourist. The tourist tried to get away when the sister placed the bundle on her back but couldn't. The sister was now anxious for them to leave.

Firingin watched and waited.

The sister led the woman to him. He saw her pull the woman's wrap to her eyes and speak with soft words.

"She wears some of my clothes," the sister said when she reached his side. "If you see people on the street, she can wrap the shawl over her hair and face. She will appear as a Moslem. I have told her."

He nodded, and the sister ushered them to the doorway. He wanted to tell her how sad he was about the trouble he had brought to her dwelling, but she quickly blew out the candle and pushed the panel aside. He took the woman by the hand and pulled her outside. Already the wail of police vehicles came from the town.

14

When Firingin came bursting through the doorway, Leslie couldn't believe how frightened he looked. He'd always been the model of courage, no matter what faced him, and now he looked terrified. He actually shouted at Maikonila when he talked to her. She shouted back, and they both talked fast and loud to each other. All the while, he kept looking at Leslie.

When she asked Maikonila what was wrong, the answer was beyond belief.

"Firingin has killed a soldier," Maikonila said. "Now the police will look for him."

Leslie stared at him. His eyes were on fire with excitement. She shuddered. How could he have done such a thing? For nearly three days, she'd admired him as one who was brave, thoughtful, and gentle. She'd even slept with him—the first man she'd ever been with in that way. Now he turned out to be a killer. She had to get away from this place. Nothing about the Samburu, or especially Firingin, made any sense.

"Why did he have to kill somebody?" she asked Maikonila.

"He did not plan it," she answered. "It was the soldier who came to attack."

Leslie covered her eyes. Perhaps she could blot it all out, for a moment at least. When she looked again, Maikonila had turned away. She'd started talking again to Firingin. He shouted even louder at her, and she started crying.

What was wrong with him? Now he was turning on his aunt. Leslie held Maikonila and glared at him. He pulled Maikonila away from Leslie and shouted again.

Maikonila sniffed back her tears.

"You can't stay here," she said to Leslie. "The police will search from house to house."

"But where will I go?"

"He wants to take you with him. To a cave he knows."

"A cave!" Leslie shouted. How could she possibly stay in a cave in Africa? She shivered. Snakes! There would be snakes. She'd seen that Indiana Jones movie. The cave had snakes everywhere. "Tell him I'm not going to any cave," she said.

Maikonila waved her hand and talked again to Firingin. Leslie wondered if she should make a break for the door. If she could make it to the street, somebody might help her. Firingin kept his eyes on her while he talked. It was hopeless.

"He says you will," Maikonila said to her. "He wants to take you there and then to the school tomorrow morning." Maikonila shook her head. "I've told him the police will be waiting, but he will not listen. He is not thinking straight, but I cannot reason with him."

Maikonila went to her room, and presently she returned with two large bags in her arms.

Leslie went to the sleeping area and watched while Firingin and Maikonila continued to argue.

They stopped and Maikonila came to her with one of the bags. She seemed to have lost the argument. Leslie tried to tell Maikonila that she couldn't go, but the woman wouldn't listen. She also seemed to have changed her mind and was now forcing Leslie to leave.

Firingin waited at the door with the other bundle already on his back. Maikonila took Leslie to him.

"Tomorrow when Firingin takes you to the school," she said, "you must try not to be recognized. The police will shoot if they see him leading a white woman." She lifted an edge of the wrap across Leslie's face. "If you do this," she continued, "they might think you're Moslem."

At the doorway, Maikonila said something to Firingin and then practically shoved him along with Leslie out of her house.

Outside, in the darkness, Leslie became desperate. She couldn't do this. She dug in her heels, but Firingin gripped her hand and pulled her. There was nobody around to yell to, and Firingin quickly moved away from the street and into the bush.

"Please come," he said and led her to a ditch surrounded by high brambles.

They slid down a short embankment, and he pulled her along the floor of the ravine. She kept trying to hold back. How could she let him take her to a cave?

Firingin persisted, and each time he jerked her hand, he said, "Please." Sometimes he said, "Please, Leslie."

Overhead, she saw a glow in the sky—probably from searchlights in the distance. She heard sounds of voices shouting. What if she simply screamed? Somebody might hear her, but Firingin could take off and leave her alone out here. Who knows who or what might find her before any police arrived.

The roar of a helicopter rose and fell over the town. Each time the chopping sound came close, Firingin dove under cover and dragged her with him. He was so vigilant and his hands were so strong, there was never a moment when she could even get free to wave.

When the sounds faded, Firingin led her back to the ravine, and after a time, they emerged on a brushy hillside. They were no longer near the town, and Leslie stopped pulling back. With God only knows what lurking in the bushes and grass, she would now stay as close as possible.

After two hours of walking and dragging the woman, Firingin finally reached the cave. It was as he remembered, a sheltered place off the trails and beyond a thicket of heavy thornbushes. It was far from a stream or water hole, and he had never seen a predator animal in the cavern.

While at school, he'd visited the cave many times with his friends. It was their special place of hiding from the schoolmasters. Many cracks in the walls of the spacious inner room allowed faint light to show in the daytime. The girls who had sometimes come with them had not been afraid, but Firingin knew that the tourist-woman was fearful. It was why she had pulled so hard against him. He quickly built a fire and spread the blankets.

She stayed close to his side, and once she asked about snakes. When he assured her that they would see none, she sat down beside the fire.

He still wanted to have sex with the woman. He wanted to feel her wild movements while he was inside.

After she watched the fire for a time, she appeared more relaxed. He sat beside her and attempted to stroke the tender inside skin of her leg. She seemed angry and pulled away.

He wanted to enter her but would not force it. The tourist woman's fearful ways fascinated him, but he did not want to be the cause of more fright. He could live for many days without sex, but he did not want to see this Leslie leave hating him.

He dug through the sister's bundles and found tea and a teapot. He poured water from his bottle, and soon the cave echoed with the sound of boiling liquid. The bubbling tea seemed to cheer the woman.

He found crackers in the bundle and also a jar of honey.

The woman smiled a weak smile when he served her the food. Later they lay on the blanket. She kept her body close to him, but he did not reach for her.

The women finally slept, and he kept watch for intruders. He thought about the sister. He liked the sister and hated to see her so fearful. She worried for the safety of her house, but he knew she also worried for him. After he returned the woman, he would go to the far side of the mountains and wait a few days. He had not been seen when he killed the soldier, so the police would soon stop their searches. Then he would go to the sister and give her his blue beads. They would help her to forget her fears and her anger. He could not return to the Samburu. He felt his failure to Lominchira, the only elder who had ever trusted him, but he also felt the sadness that his failure had brought to the Samburu people. Maybe someday, many seasons from now, they could forget his failure. Then he might be allowed to once more herd the beasts with the children. Until then, he would have to live like an abandoned hyena, outside the family.

He thought of the sister's words about him being discovered when he returned the woman. The sister did not know that he had a plan. In the darkness, he would first locate the nighttime sentries around the school.

There would be only a few—the police slept like all the other people. He would then stay in the shadows of the buildings while he took Leslie to the porch of the medical clinic. He would leave her there, and she could talk to the doctors when they came. The doctors all spoke English. If the police saw her before the doctors arrived, she could pretend to be a Moslem woman waiting for treatment.

It was a good plan, but only if they went in the dark. He stoked the fire high and curled up for a short period of sleep.

When Firingin awakened, the cave was dark. The fire had burned out. He ran to the opening of the cave and checked the sky. The sun's glow had not appeared on the horizon. He woke the woman and lit the fire. He made tea and millet with honey for their breakfast.

While they ate, the woman kept looking at him. Her eyes sparkled from light of the flames.

"I take you back now," he told her.

She stared at him and said nothing.

Perhaps she did not understand his Swahili. "Take you to the school," he said.

She shook her head. "Maikonila said the police will be waiting," she said. The tourist woman had learned some Swahili words at the sister's dwelling. "Bang! Bang!" the woman said. She made motions like one shooting a weapon.

He laughed and waved his hands. "There is no problem." The woman did not know of his plan. Suddenly, she leaned her body toward him and used her arms to hug him. He started to pull back, but her eyes showed sadness. He sat still and felt his desire for her grow.

This woman was indeed strange. Last night she resisted, but now she seemed to want him.

"Come," she said. She patted a place beside her.

He moved to the spot and waited. He wanted her sex, but he would not frighten her.

The woman opened the front of her wrap, and he could see the tops of her breasts. Below the line where the sun had browned her, the skin was pale and smooth like the cream of a goat. He touched her, and she didn't object. He removed his loin wrap and his jewelry. He wanted to feel her skin against his when he entered her.

The woman removed the cloth from her body and lay back, pushing her nipples high. He placed her for entry from the rear, and she looked back at him and smiled with her eyes. He liked this strange woman.

When he entered her, she writhed as she had before. This time she screamed when he was inside. He held her breasts, but it only calmed her a little. Sex with this Leslie was the best he'd ever known.

15

Leslie had no idea how he had found the cave. In the dark, it looked like any other wall of rock, covered with brambles and bushes. Inside, she waited, almost numb with terror, while Firingin built a fire.

Anemic flames cast shadows over the cave's walls, and she thought of what might be aroused by the moving patterns. She made a sweeping motion with her hand.

"Snakes?" she said.

He smiled and shook his head. "I chase them away."

She believed him. What choice did she have?

She sat on a blanket as close as she could get to the growing flames. She'd heard in Campfire Girls that a fire was one of the best ways to keep creepy things at bay.

Firingin sat down beside her. She didn't mind at first; his nearness seemed to be the only real protection she had. Then he started stroking her leg!

She couldn't believe it. Against her will, he'd dragged her over rocks and through thornbushes, brought her to this terrifying cave, and now he wanted to make love just like nothing had happened.

"No!" she said and pushed his hand away.

It didn't seem to bother him. He simply stopped.

He stood and picked up one of the bundles. He dug in it a moment and pulled out a pot and a small package.

"Tea," he said.

She sat huddled on the blanket. When the water boiled, it made a cheerful sound. It was the first pleasant thing she'd experienced since last night.

After a snack, she curled up close to him—but not touching. The warmth of the fire and her physical and emotional exhaustion conspired, and she fell asleep.

"Leslie." She heard Firingin's voice and felt his hand on her shoulder. She opened her eyes and saw nothing. The panic of disorientation gripped her until she remembered where she was. Then a different panic took over.

Desperate for protection, she reached for him.

"Please build a fire," she said.

"Soon," he replied. She heard rustling sounds. How could he see?

A match flickered, and she saw his face over it.

With attentive eyes, he looked into the glow—she nearly cried. He looked so gentle. How could he have killed someone?

Flames burst from the wood, and Firingin busied himself with the teapot.

They ate a breakfast of grains and honey. She watched him while he ate. He was a fascinating man. He seemed to always know what he was doing. It was a quality that now made her feel completely safe, even in this African cave. She thought of the way he'd callously touched her leg the night before. It had seemed so insensitive, but then he'd immediately withdrawn when she objected. He must not have realized how terrifying it was for her to be here. Now she felt a little guilty about the entire episode.

He gathered the dishes and stuffed them into one of the bags. "Take you back now," he announced.

It was what Maikonila had said he would do. But she'd also said the police would be waiting and that they would shoot if they saw him with Leslie.

"Take you to the school," he said.

How could he even think of going back there? The town had been crawling with police, and all of them were looking for him.

What would she do if they shot him right in front of her? "Maikonila said the police would be waiting," she said. She made shooting motions for emphasis.

He actually laughed.

In the dim light of the cave, she regarded him. He must, indeed, be the bravest man she had ever known. The thought of him risking his life for her brought tears to her eyes once again. Impulsively, she leaned over and hugged him.

She didn't care about last night. It was obviously a cultural thing. She had to feel him close to her, once more, before she left. She wanted him to know, before it was too late, that she really did care for him.

She patted a place on the blanket. With him nakedness was ordinary, but she opened the top of her wrap anyhow.

With unbelievable anticipation, she watched while he removed his knife belt, his jewelry, and his loin cloth.

When he stretched out beside her, she could scarcely contain herself. Except for the circular sections of bone in his ear lobes, he was completely naked.

She removed her wrap and laid it aside. His hands moved to her waist. Strong and gentle, they picked her up and turned her over. With her face away from him, she felt him spread her legs. He touched her breasts. Her nipples tingled, and she felt the pressure grow as he moved inside. She matched his motions and closed her eyes against the rolling releases.

A few minutes after they'd made love, he told her, once again, that it was time to go. So much for relaxing after sex. She protested again about danger from the police, but he assured her that he would not take risks.

They traveled for nearly half an hour from the cave to a ravine that Firingin said would lead to the school.

The light was still dim so Leslie couldn't see much, but it wasn't dark by any means. She wondered if he would still go ahead if it became daylight.

Birds were everywhere in the shrubs and trees. The African birds had the most melodious songs in the morning that Leslie had ever heard. The grass along their path to the ravine had been wet with dew. The lower part of Leslie's wrap had been soaked, but she didn't mind. She'd felt wonderfully serene while they'd been walking from the cave, but now her thoughts were engulfed in sadness. Soon she would be leaving him.

She shook her head. But it had to be. If she stayed, she would only cause him trouble. He needed to escape from the police, and her sore feet would just slow him down. She couldn't stay anyhow. Eventually he'd go back to his Samburu village. She knew she couldn't live in such a place; she'd have asthma attacks all the time.

At least she would have her memories. She smiled to herself. She would never forget the days and the nights she had spent with him.

Her reverie was broken by his touch on her arm. He motioned her to keep low. They must be getting close to the school. She bent over and followed him across a stretch where the bushes were short. She looked over her shoulder at the hills behind them and saw the sun beginning to appear.

Firingin stopped. The buildings were just beyond the opposite bank. She heard voices, but Firingin said nothing. He motioned for her to wait, and he crept to the other side of the ravine. She watched from the bushes while he raised his head for a look. He ducked back, and she saw him flatten against the ground.

When he crawled back to her, he looked worried.

Firingin led Leslie back to the beginning of the ravine. There it was safe to speak.

"I cannot return you today," he said. "The soldiers are many."

She nodded. "Yes, I heard them."

He motioned for her to follow him. They would return to the cave. He hoped she wouldn't be so fearful this time.

It was not dark in the cavern, but he built up the fire anyhow. The smoke would go to a deeper part of the cave.

"What will we do now?" she asked. The woman worried more than he did.

"In another day they might leave," he answered.

She shook her head. "More will come."

"Tomorrow I will take you when it is still dark. It was too light this morning."

"Even in the darkness, soldiers will be there," she said. Again, she made shooting motions.

He poked the fire. What she said was true. More soldiers will surround the school, and they will soon also search the hills. They will find the cave.

He walked to the entrance to think without her questions.

When it grew dark, he and the woman would have to leave.

He looked over his shoulder at her. He could not go without her. Even if he wanted to, she would fear being left in the cave.

He would take the sister's advice and go to Parsaloi. He and Leslie could wait there. He would listen to talk in the town until he heard that the police had given up. They would search longer now, because of Leslie, but they would someday tire. Then he would bring Leslie back to the school. By then, the headmaster would be there. He could take her to her people.

Firingin smiled, pleased with the simplicity of his plan. It would not bring the restoration of his status, but Leslie would be safely returned.

He knelt by the fire. "When night comes, we will go across the mountains," he told her.

Her eyes widened. "Mountains!" she said.

She rubbed one of her feet. "Where will we go?"

"We must go far," he said. "We will wait in a distant place for the soldiers to leave."

The woman's body shivered. He stared at the fire, and she poured herself a cup of tea. She drank quickly and placed the cup by the fire. They sat together, and she pressed her body close. He stroked her leg, and she didn't object.

16

When Firingin talked of trying again at the school, Leslie couldn't believe it. Why was he so intent on getting himself killed?

She watched from the blanket while he walked to the cave entrance. He stared outside for a long time. She wondered if he had heard something. Then he came back to the fire and sat down.

When he told her they would start in the dark and go over some mountains, she felt herself cringe. How could she handle Firingin's fast walking in the mountains?

Even with the car-tire sandals Maikonila had given her, she wouldn't last long.

But there was no question about him having to go somewhere. If the police in Kenya were anything like those in America, troops would soon be swarming all over the place.

She wondered where this would all end. He'd said they would wait over the mountains for the police to leave. When would that be? She wished she knew the words to ask him.

One thing was certain—she couldn't stay in this cave by herself.

She sat close to him and tried to imagine them having a real conversation. How wonderful it would be to share their thoughts and feelings, to find out how he felt about her. She knew so little. He was strong and resourceful, a man who had killed a snake in a flash and even a soldier, but what went on in his mind? Did he feel remorse over the soldier? He seemed so caring, but yet he could be so stern. She wondered about his family. Except for Maikonila, she hadn't met any of them—unless some of the people that first day were his bothers or sisters. Maybe the man with the Yankees' ball cap was his father. It was strange. In some ways she knew Firingin better than any man in the world, but still she knew almost nothing about him as a person.

His hands stroked her leg. She wouldn't resist. It was their best way of communicating.

"Go now," Firingin said.

She sat up and rubbed her eyes. Through the entrance of the cave, she saw the gold of a sky at sunset.

The fire's flames licked at a blackened stew pot.

He already had something cooking.

"Eat first," he said. "Then, we go."

He handed her a portion and she stirred the thick mixture. "This looks familiar," she said.

He pointed to a box and grinned. It was oatmeal.

Maikonila must have emptied her cupboard. They ate then and Firingin packed the bundles while Leslie attempted to clean her contacts. He tied the smaller bundle to her back, and they stepped into the shadowy twilight.

Soon the glow of a star-filled sky lit their way along a narrow but well-traveled trail. Firingin made an upward motion with his hand. He swept his arm through an arc, tracing the peak in front of them.

"Kisima mountain," he said. "We climb."

She nodded. His need to tell her where they were going was touching, but it didn't make the ache in her feet any less intense.

The ascent on the rocky pathway was difficult, more tiring than the trek they had taken from the Samburu village to Maralal, but it wouldn't do her any good to complain. She had no choice but to stay with him.

Each time they stopped to rest, Firingin unsheathed his knife. He held his weapon at the ready and only put it away when they resumed the trek. After the first stop, she noticed that he constantly rubbed the knife's handle. The process seemed to make him thoughtful, and he kept glancing at the handle, even when he was walking.

She wished he could tell her what bothered him. If it was remorse over killing the soldier, she would like to help him deal with it. Maikonila had told her it was self defense. Maybe he needed somebody to let him know he wasn't to blame.

Leslie shivered. She wondered if the events of the last few days had somehow affected her own sanity. How could she help him? No rational woman would be traveling alone on this remote African mountain with a man she couldn't even talk to. She didn't even know their destination.

The horizon had begun to glow with the sunrise when Firingin and Leslie finally started downward on the trail. They had stopped often, but her legs and feet were throbbing with pain.

After a short descent, she and Firingin entered a forested area. Canopies of acacias hung over their heads, and cast dark shadows on the pathway.

Leslie heard the distant "hoo-woup" of a prowling hyena. She had heard the same sound when the tour group was in the

Masaai Mara. Calvin had told them it was the most frequent sound a hyena makes. The giggling that they always do in the movies only happens in real-life when hyenas fight.

The cry of the hyena stopped, and Leslie recognized screams of a ravaged troop of baboons. An African forest at night seemed to never be quiet for long.

Firingin paid little attention to the faraway sounds. He walked solemnly, always looking. When they approached a low-hanging limb, he signaled a halt.

He pointed to where the morning light revealed a thick appendage dangling from the branch.

"Leopard!" he whispered. She saw the animal's tail twitch with anticipation, and Firingin nudged her back.

He directed her around the tree, and when they were back on the trail he spoke.

"His tail moved. He had not eaten for a long time."

"You think he was waiting for us?"

"I think so." Firingin smiled. "He will have to wait longer for his meal."

She shuddered. She wanted to say thank you, but Firingin had already started down the trail.

When they reached the bottom of the slope, he directed her off the trail. After an hour's hike through heavy brush, he signaled another stop.

Before them lay a shaded area that was covered with short, well-groomed grass.

"We stay here," he said and started building a fire.

"Why is the grass so short here?" she asked.

He looked up from his work and frowned. She moved her arms to sweep the area and then reached down to the grass. Firingin smiled. "Gazelles," he said. "They feed here."

"That will be nice," she said.

"Sometimes cheetah feed on gazelles," he said. "I will chase."

She watched him work until he motioned to one of the bundles. She took the hint and unpacked the cereal and some pomegranates for breakfast.

After they ate, Firingin cut branches from a nearby thicket and formed them into a low hut. It looked much like the hovel she'd stayed in at the village.

He carried rocks inside for a fireplace and spread his cape over the roof.

Finally, he came to where she sat on one of the blankets. He sat beside her and smiled. "Our dwelling," he said.

This was apparently where they would wait for the police to leave. She went inside for an inspection. As expected it was sparse, but the smell was fresh.

When she emerged, Firingin pointed to a nearby stream. It was such a small trickle, she hadn't before noticed it.

He started making swimming motions with his arms.

She had to laugh. How could he expect to swim there?

He dug through one of the bundles and came up with a bar of soap. He walked toward the trickle, and she followed. This would be something to see.

They walked a distance along the bank. The stream widened and then narrowed to an even smaller flow. They rounded a bend and came upon a dam made of fallen rocks.

Firingin ran ahead, flailing the bank with branches.

He grinned and made more swimming motions. Leslie followed him to the other side of the dam. There he flailed the shore around a knee-deep pool of clear water.

"Spring," he said. "We wash."

"Is it safe?"

Firingin nodded. "I chase everything away."

He removed his clothes and waded in with the bar of soap in his hand. She didn't want to stay alone on the shore, so she undressed and cautiously entered the basin. He stared shamelessly.

She felt embarrassed. "Don't," she said.

He smiled but kept looking. She sat down in the water and slapped a spray at his eyes. He grabbed her, and they splashed and laughed like two children. She forgot all about her sore feet and the dangers.

When the pool filled with suds, they got out and laid on a grassy part of the bank.

The air was warm, and they had sex under the open sky.

Later, they returned to the campsite, a modern-day Adam and Eve, completely nude with their clothes tucked under their arms.

After they dressed, Firingin stood near the outside fireplace and drank a cup of tea. Leslie sat on the blanket and watched him.

His right hand drifted to the handle of his knife.

Again he was deep in thought.

17

Cross-legged, Firingin stood on the sandy river bank and surveyed the scene before him. He'd visited the Milgis Lugga Basin once as a child, but that had been years earlier. In the moonlight, the valley seemed even more expansive than he remembered it.

Leslie sat at the edge of a meandering thread of the stream and soaked her feet. She'd complained about them hurting since the beginning of the trek, and even with the ten-day stay at the forest camp, they had not recovered.

She turned around and smiled. He smiled back. In spite of her slow walking and finicky ways, he had grown fond of the tourist woman. Every day she wanted his sex, and he enjoyed giving it to her. She wasn't sexy to look at—her breasts were too small—but she was definitely inviting on the blankets.

A shriek rang out from a grove across the river, and Leslie jumped to her feet. She limped to Firingin's side and grabbed his arm.

"Only a hyrax," he said.

She dropped her grip. "I'm sorry. I should be getting used to them."

He grinned. Her sentence had used several of the Swahili words they'd been practicing.

"I like you in spite of your fears," he said.

"And I like you too." She jumped up and kissed his mouth! He wiped his lips. He'd never had such a thing done to him.

He leaned down to let her do it again. It felt nice. He laughed, and Leslie laughed, too.

She hopped on one leg back to the edge of the river and resumed her foot bathing. She started to sing one of her English songs. It sounded cheerful.

Leslie had seemed joyous ever since they left the camp. She was, no doubt, happy that she would soon be going back to her people.

He would not be going now. He hadn't told her, but it had become unsafe for him to ever return to Maralal or even his home village.

His fingers drifted to the handle of his knife and to the band at its base. They moved until they touched the jagged edge of the cavity. He'd explored it dozens of times since he made the discovery.

The answer was the same. The ruby was gone. He had looked everywhere—through his clothes, through Leslie's wrap while she'd slept, and through the bundles of the sister's things.

There could be no other explanation. The jewel had jarred loose when the knife had struck the soldier's back. The police would find it and would soon use it to connect him with the stabbing. They would ask Samburus about it.

They would ask Samburus about the ruby, and eventually,

the elder who gave him the knife would be questioned.

When Firingin thought of Lominchira, he closed his eyes against the pain. The torment of failing the old one's trust had grown strong in Firingin's heart. The man who had honored him would now suffer from the police because of him.

Leslie stopped singing and came to Firingin's side. "What's the matter?" she said.

He shrugged. He would not tell her about such complications.

"It is time to go," he said.

"Can't we rest a little longer?" She sat down on the sand and rubbed one of her feet. "This one still hurts."

He picked up the remaining bundle and handed it to Leslie. "Hold this," he said. "I will carry you."

On the morning of the twelfth day after leaving Maralal, Firingin made camp behind a large grove of riverside trees. He'd selected a site which was well hidden, because around the next bend of the river stood the village of Parsaloi.

He cleared brush from the area under an overhanging acacia and spread the blankets. While he worked, Leslie removed her wrap and curled herself next to the fire. After a full night of riding on his shoulders, she would be rested and eager to play.

He regarded her smooth skin, glowing with the fire's warmth, and felt the temptation.

He would not submit. All of the grain from the sister had been eaten. He needed to hunt game for the breakfast.

"I must go," he said. "The prey will soon sleep in the burrows."

Leslie looked sad, but he remained strong. He cut a stout club for her to use as a protective weapon and slipped into the thicket behind the camp.

He made a wide sweep of the brushy hills away from the river but didn't see any acceptable targets. Snakes and small birds were plentiful, but Leslie refused to eat their meat.

He climbed a gentle mound and heard a rustling sound on the other side. He peeked over the thorn-bushes and saw a flock of guineafowl scratching and clucking in an open area. One of those gourd-sized creatures would make a satisfying meal, even for Leslie.

He selected a fat hen at the edge of the group and crept from behind the bushes. The flock spooked and flew in a flurry of stubby wings.

He pursued them, and when he saw his target scurrying toward dense underbrush, he threw his knife.

End over end it flew, but he was not familiar with the blade's balance. His weapon struck a hand's width from the bird. The guineafowl flushed to safe cover. Firingin needed a less agile target.

Another half hour passed before he saw a likely candidate. A large African hare hopped slowly, grazing from blade to blade on the dry grass.

Firingin moved in, and the animal dashed under a bush. There it froze, still as a rock.

Firingin crept to close range and with a lightning thrust, ended the creature's deception.

He skinned the animal and ran at full speed toward the campsite. He worried about leaving Leslie alone for such a long time. She had survived nearly two weeks on the trail and in their camps, but she had not gained in courage.

He arrived after a twenty minute run and found her sitting straight and alert in the middle of the blankets.

She stared at the far side of the clearing and didn't turn to look at him.

He wondered if she might be looking away because she remained unhappy about him leaving. Such foolishness would make him angry.

He scanned in the direction of her stare and quickly saw that she didn't look away because of spite.

A silver-backed jackal gazed back from the far edge of the clearing. With its nose placed on outstretched forepaws and mischief in its eyes, the creature mirrored Leslie's glare.

Apparently still unaware of Firingin, Leslie shook her club at the animal. The jackal yawned its contempt, and that made him laugh out loud.

The creature looked in his direction and, with frantic speed, jumped and darted away.

Leslie looked around. She seemed surprised to see him and also embarrassed. She stretched in an obvious attempt to appear casual. "He's been here since just after you left," she said.

"It was a jackal. Such a small animal would never hurt someone so fierce as you."

She laughed. He liked her laugh.

He held up the skinned carcass of their breakfast.

She made a strange face. "Yuk! What is it?"

"An African hare. Its meat is good." He knelt beside the fire and fanned it to flames.

Leslie placed her cheek on his shoulder. "Can't we wait for breakfast?" she said.

"The meat will spoil."

She seemed angry again and crawled to the far side of the blanket.

Leslie said nothing while he prepared the food. He was puzzled by her demanding nature. A Samburu wife would never be so bold with her needs. He smiled. Why had he thought of Leslie as a wife?

The meat made a good smell as it cooked, and Leslie ate a large helping. Later they had the sex. She rocked as hard as ever when he was inside. It pleased him that she could forget her anger so quickly.

When they relaxed on the blankets, Leslie sat close to him. "I'm sorry I was so *selfish*," she said.

Her last word was in English. She used English words often with her Swahili.

"Sell fish?" he asked. "I do not understand." He dug in the bag and found the tablet and pencil. "Please, draw."

She shook her head. "I can't." She looked sad.

"Why are you unhappy?"

"I can't tell you. We just don't have the words. You can't draw feelings."

He said nothing.

"Soon I'll be going back," she said, "and we never have really talked." Tears showed in her eyes.

She patted his hand and sniffed back her tears. "I'm going to miss you," she said.

Her talk of missing him made him ashamed. He was not sure if he would miss her. He did like many things about her, but he had always known that she would go away. He had kept himself from feeling too close to her. He tried to make her talk. "We may have many days before a caravan comes," he said.

She wiped her eyes. "Caravan? What do you mean by that word?"

It was one they had not practiced, so he drew a picture on the tablet.

"Oh, camels," she said.

"Camels," he repeated. "You will ride one to Maralal."

"Ride a camel! Now that should be fun. Like *Lawrence of Arabia*."

He had no idea what her last words meant, but was glad she had stopped crying.

"I will go across to the town and ask some of the people," he said. "But you must wait here."

"Town? What town?" She stood and walked in a circle. "Have I been asleep or what?"

He motioned for her to sit down. "You cannot see the town," he said. "It is beyond the next turn in the river. On the other side."

She sat and looked at him. "So when will you go see this place?"

"Tonight. I will use darkness to keep me hidden."

"Why? You think there are police around?"

"I do not think so, but I must be sure before I enter Parsaloi."

"That's the name of this place? Parsaloi?"

He couldn't believe how curious she'd become.

"Yes, Parsaloi," he answered. "It is a small town. A crossroads for caravans."

"But won't they know you're a Samburu?"

"I will remove all of my jewelry," he said. "If the police do not see me close, they will think I am Rendille."

Leslie laughed. "You're a *sly* one," she said. "I had no idea we were so close to a town." She had used an English word again, but he wouldn't ask her to draw it.

18

When Leslie returned to the bank of the river, she sat down and started singing. "Michael Row the Boat Ashore" would be a good song to take away her fears, and besides, she felt like singing. Firingin had actually enjoyed it when she'd kissed him. At first, he hadn't seemed to understand what she was doing, but then he'd leaned over for another.

She couldn't believe how she was acting—like a girl in high school with him, but a much different girl than she had been herself.

She thought about her pending return to civilization. Last night, when she and Firingin had left the forest camp, he'd told her that they would reach a town in a few days. From there, he'd said, she'd go back to Maralal. She'd wondered why he'd said that she, not they, would be going. It must have been his way of expressing it, because he'd said before that he would be bringing her back.

The last two weeks had been the most grueling ordeal of her life, but she still felt sad when she thought about leaving him. During their ten-day stay in the forest, she had grown even more attached to Firingin.

In some ways, his care had reminded her of the nurturing she'd received from her Aunt Jean. He hadn't always been gentle like Aunt Jean, but he'd never failed to provide for Leslie's needs and her safety. In the forest camp, he had worked tirelessly to keep all the creepy things away.

The only creatures she had seen around their makeshift dwelling had been bugs and several small lizards. She had seen but one snake. It was the one he had brought back, skinned, from one of his hunting expeditions. He'd wanted to roast it for dinner, but she'd quickly made it plain that she'd never dream of eating snake meat.

Except for the sex, which they'd had often, the camp had been basically a boring place. The tedium of each day had been relieved only a little by Firingin's comical attempts to teach her Swahili. Every morning after breakfast, he had solemnly recited a list of words and asked her to identify the represented objects. His pompous manner must have been to impose his teacher's authority on her. Sometimes he'd painstakingly draw the object for the word on his tablet, and she would have to laugh. Each day he'd added more words, and now she could talk to him about almost all the objects and things she saw. Thoughts and feelings were still difficult.

She looked over her shoulder to where he stood on the bank. She noticed that he had, again, placed his hand on the knife. This time his eyes were closed. It was as if he were suffering an intense pain.

She got up and hopped on one foot to his side. When she asked him what was wrong, he didn't answer. He simply looked at her and said that it was time to start walking. When she couldn't because of the soreness in her feet, he picked her up and carried her.

He carried her the rest of that night and all of the next. The banks along the wide, mainly dry, river were level, so she didn't feel too guilty about riding on his shoulders.

He walked in silence, never singing.

In the moonlight, it seemed she could see for miles along the broad valley. She liked looking at the scenery. It was so open. Only trees along the banks and low mountains in the background broke the serenity of the view.

Occasionally in the distance, she saw other travelers. Whenever they appeared, Firingin walked directly to a nearby thicket. There he waited until whoever it was left the area. He seemed worried about being seen, even after all the time they'd been hiding.

On the morning after their second night on the river trail, they stopped under a grove of large trees.

While Firingin cleared brush from the campsite, Leslie built the fire. His enthusiasm made her think that this might be their final camp.

She spread a blanket near the fire, and the heat of the flames felt good in the morning coolness. She gazed at the familiar movements of Firingin's body while he worked. She felt a tingle of anticipated sex.

Riding on his shoulders all night had definitely developed her interest.

She removed her wrap. The sight of her without clothing usually got his attention.

He finished his work and walked to the fireplace.

Instead of lying down beside her, he handed her a large stick and said he had to go hunting for their breakfast.

She felt stung by his rejection. Perhaps they'd been together too long.

He left, and she fumbled through the bundle for the tablet. She'd started keeping a journal of her experiences. Inside the bag, she found a container of cooked rice that was left from yesterday afternoon's meal. She nibbled a little, but it tasted stale. She tossed out the remainder.

A few minutes later, she saw a jackal sniffing at the rice. It didn't eat but laid down at the edge of the clearing. She had no idea what it wanted and shouted for it to go. It didn't move. She picked up the club Firingin had left and shook it. Still the jackal remained. Leslie set up a vigil. If the jackal wouldn't leave, she would have to watch it.

When Firingin returned from his hunt, he laughed at her standoff. It must have been a strange sight indeed for him to see her and the big-eared animal glaring at each other like a couple of gunfighters.

After breakfast, which was rabbit meat and not too bad, Firingin finally did come to her. He seemed as interested as ever, but she still tried to make it good.

With probably just another day left together, she didn't want her memories to be spoiled.

He seemed satisfied and afterward they talked. It was then he told her about the camels. She hadn't known before how they'd be going back. She'd thought maybe it would be in a native bus, one of those colorful contraptions she'd seen with the tour group.

He said he'd go to a town called Parsaloi and make arrangements with a caravan. He told her that the town was just up the river, and he'd go that evening. It would be the first time he would leave her alone at night. He said he needed the darkness for cover. Still, it terrified her.

For his trip to the town, Firingin wore only his sandals and the wrap around his waist. He told Leslie that he didn't want someone to see him dressed as a Samburu.

His caution puzzled her. Maikonila had said that nobody had seen him kill the soldier, so after hiding so many days in the forest, why did he continue to worry about the police?

"I will not be away for a long time," he said.

She tried to look brave but knew she couldn't.

He'd piled a giant stack of firewood near the blankets. "Keep the flames high," he said. "The camp is well hidden from the river. No one should see. If some people come, wrap your face."

She laughed a forced laugh but said nothing. Her voice would have been shaky.

19

Firingin's heart pounded with excitement when he stopped across the river from Parsaloi. Its collection of huts and low central buildings were close enough now to be easily visible in the moonless light. He would watch for a time to be sure that no soldier-patrols were present. No people in the town would know him. He did not anticipate seeing any Samburu in Parsaloi. They were a people too proud to tolerate the rough talk of camel drivers.

Over an hour passed, and he waited. He thought of sending Leslie back. It would be difficult. He had never known a woman so receptive to him. Sometimes her desire for sex interfered with the duties of his life, but still he found her compelling. She was interesting to talk to and being with such a woman had shown him what it could be like to live as an adult. More than ever he wished for his status. But it would not be. Even if he could avoid capture, the Samburus would not accept him back. The father had used many curses on him by now. Firingin wondered where he would go. Perhaps when the woman was on her way, he would continue north.

There had been no sign of soldiers or police near the town. The moon would soon light the valley, so he would make his entrance while darkness remained.

Slowly, he waded the shallow river and then walked directly to the center of town. He would ask about the caravan and hurry back to Leslie. He had given her much wood for the fire, but she was afraid.

The watering trough in front of one of the main buildings would be where the caravans stopped. A lone camel near the trough raised its head and gave him a sleepy look.

Firingin bent over the spout that fed spring water and cupped his hands for a drink. It tasted good, and he filled his bottle.

Two people huddled in blankets near a wall of the building. They talked in Swahili, and Firingin hunkered down to listen.

"From where do you come?" one man asked.

"My family is in the North," Firingin answered.

"Better than the South," the man said.

Firingin nodded. "It's bad there?"

"Bad. Soldiers search all the villages for a murderer. Haven't you heard of this?"

Firingin tried to think of a good response. "I have been hunting in the mountains," he said. "Now I seek a caravan to Maralal."

"Maralal! It is not possible. No caravans go there."

"How can that be?" Firingin asked. "Maralal is a center for trade."

"This is true," the man said, "but no caravans can come out of there without being searched. The drivers from the North take their goods to Ngilai or Wamba."

Firingin shook his head and stood to leave. He could have asked more questions, but he'd heard enough. He needed to return to Leslie.

"Maybe you should go back to the North," the man said.

"It is possible that I will," Firingin said. Before anyone else could speak, he slipped into the darkness.

The site was dark when Firingin approached it. It surprised him that Leslie had let the fire go out.

"Leslie," he whispered.

No answer.

He hurried to the blankets, and he heard her moan. A mound of bedding lay near the fireplace.

"Leslie," he said again. He shook the mound. "Don't be afraid."

She pushed an edge of blanket away from her face. Even in the shadows, he could see her teeth chatter. She spoke, but he could not understand her.

It was the most terrifying feeling of Leslie's life. She had watched Firingin walk out of the clearing and now sat alone, at night, in the African wilds. There was only one consolation—it would probably be the only time she would have to do this. Tomorrow they'd be on their way back.

She threw a handful of wood on the fire and sat as close as possible to the flames.

A tree hyrax started screeching. Leslie shivered.

How could she endure this? The brush around the campsite literally crawled with sounds.

Her palms became sweaty and her mouth went completely dry. She took a drink from the leftover water she'd boiled earlier to make saline solution for her contacts.

The dryness in her mouth remained.

She was shivering constantly, and when she put more sticks on the fire, she couldn't even hold a handful.

Somehow she had to get a grip on herself. She tried singing. Her voice came out low and husky. She started several songs and settled on "There Is No Problem." If someone heard the Swahili ditty, they might not get suspicious.

She saw reflected light from a pair of eyes at the edge of the thicket. She stopped singing and froze.

Using all the courage she could muster, she sidestepped to the woodpile. She needed to build up the fire. While she completed the task, she kept the glowing spots constantly in view. The animal didn't move, and she concluded that it was the jackal. Even as lights in the night, the eyes from her stand-off had a familiar look.

Somehow the jackal gave her comfort. She'd survived him before, and perhaps his presence would scare away other animals.

She couldn't stop shivering. Even her stomach had started to churn. She decided to curl up in the blankets.

No sooner had she covered herself than she had to quickly dismantle her nest. An attack of nausea forced her to crawl away from the blankets.

She wretched and up came her last meals. Her body shuddered. *This is crazy*, she thought. *Now, I'm so scared I'm throwing up.*

Back at the fire, she curled up again. She checked the jackal. He was still there. She closed her eyes.

She dozed but again became nauseous.

The next time she threw up and crawled back to the fire, she was so weak she just burrowed under the blankets and shivered.

The night became an eternity of crawling back and forth between the dwindling fire and the edge of the blankets. She hadn't the strength to put on more wood.

Her fear had vanished. It had been replaced by a determination not to throw up again. Her stomach must have already turned inside out. Nothing but rasping croaks came out.

Finally she slept.

She dreamt dreams of trying to get away from something, a shapeless threat in the darkness. She moaned for her Aunt Jean. Aunt Jean would have made it better if she had only come.

Leslie began to dream merging images of Aunt Jean and Firingin. She cried for help—she didn't get a response from either. She was soaked with perspiration, a condition she sensed during the momentary awakenings between her dreams.

When she felt the shake of her shoulder, she recoiled. Then she heard Firingin's voice.

She pushed back the cover and raised her head. Her stomach rebelled, and she fell back.

She told him she was sick and covered herself with the soaked bedding.

Sunlight through the tree limbs forced Leslie's eyes open. It was daylight. She felt Firingin's arms supporting her, and she smiled a weak smile.

"Can you eat?" he said.

"No!"

He looked puzzled. She repeated the answer in Swahili.

He nodded and laid her back on the blankets. She went to sleep.

The next time she woke, he was still there.

"How long have you been sitting here?" she asked.

He shrugged. "Last night when I came back, you were hot." He felt her forehead. "You are cooler now."

She smiled. "Nobody has felt my head like that for a long time."

He went to the fireplace and poured a cup of tea. He held it toward her.

She held up her hands. "I'll take some water though."

He brought her a bowl. "It is from the spring at Parsaloi."

She drank. She'd never tasted better water.

She fell asleep again, and when she awoke the next time, she felt stronger.

It was dark, and he was by the fire. Its light showed concern on his face.

She reached and patted his arm. "I'm glad you're here," she said. "Have you been watching me all day?"

He smiled. "I like you, Leslie. I must not let you die."

It might have been her weakness, but she felt tears.

"I don't think I'll die," she said. "I may never eat cooked rice again, but I'll live."

"Can you eat soup?"

"I'll try."

He went to the fireplace and dipped liquid from the stew pot. "When you slept, I killed a guinea fowl. The soup is from its meat."

She managed a smile. "Chicken soup," she said.

He shrugged and handed her the bowl.

She sat up and ate. "What about the camels?" she asked.

He shook his head. "They do not go to Maralal. The police stop them."

"Stop them? But it's nearly two weeks since the soldier was..." She stopped. She just couldn't say the rest.

He said nothing.

"So how will we get back?" she asked.

"We cannot go now."

"We can't stay here," she said. "I hate this place."

He nodded. "It is also possible that this camp will not stay hidden."

"I hope you're not thinking of walking back."

He shook his head. "Police may be on the trails."

"They sure are aggressive."

He shrugged. He did that a lot.

"What then will we do?" she said.

"Perhaps we should take a caravan to the North. I have people in Rendille country."

Leslie nodded. "Maikonila told me about them."

"They will keep us until the police have given up their searches."

Leslie wondered how long that might be. She wasn't sure if she could handle another native village, but she didn't seem to have many choices.

"I will wait until you are well before I go back to the town."

"I won't stay here again alone at night," she said. "Can't you go in the daytime?"

He nodded. "I will try."

21

Firingin heard the camels bellowing long before they were visible. People around the building woke up from their heat-induced naps and moved toward the sounds. The caravan came in from the North, so it would leave in a southeasterly direction. Firingin and Leslie would not join it.

The beasts surrounded the water trough, and the dusty men of the desert climbed over the animals' backs and tried to maintain order. Firingin stood nearby and watched the drivers' frantic efforts. It took much cursing and yelling to keep the unruly creatures from dislodging the loads when they pushed and shoved toward the springwater.

In time, the camels quenched their thirst and settled into a reasonably congenial community.

A leather-faced driver smoked near the water trough, and one of the waiting travelers advanced to ask a question.

"Will you be adding passengers?" the man asked.

The driver regarded the traveler with the scorn of an instant superior and issued a curt reply. "Our beasts are loaded with salt," he said. "We can't carry anything more."

Several people left to reclaim their places in the shade. Firingin stayed. Another driver filled his flask at the waterspout. The man asked if anyone had heard about police patrols in the South.

No one volunteered an answer.

"We've heard rumors everywhere between here and Banissa about the hunt for a Samburu," the driver offered. "Some say the army is searching the hills north of Maralal."

None of the travelers responded to his bait. The transients of Parsaloi were interested in getting a ride to somewhere else—nothing more.

The camel drivers reloaded the animals, and Firingin went back to the building. The people waiting in Parsaloi had begun to accept him, so he decided to linger awhile longer. Perhaps during the middle of the day another caravan would come in.

A traveler standing near the door to the building spoke skeptically of the driver's comments. "That camel herder knows nothing," the man said. "Maralal was as quiet as a tomb when I left."

Firingin looked at the speaker. The man seemed better dressed than the other transients. Also, his Swahili had the smooth sound of an educated Kenyan. Who was he? Why hadn't Firingin noticed him before?

"When did you leave Maralal?" another man asked.

"Two days ago," the man answered.

Firingin grew apprehensive. The man's talk of quiet in Maralal was unbelievable, maybe a trick. Could he be from the police? Firingin would not wait to find out.

He drifted away from the group and headed for the river. Before he crossed, he traveled a distance beyond the town. On the other side, he stayed behind the trees until he reached the camp.

Leslie was asleep. After her sickness, she had rarely left the blankets.

He'd hated to leave her that morning, but after waiting around the campsite for two days, he'd begun to worry. Now it seemed his concern about the police had been justified.

He shook her awake, and she sat up. She rubbed her eyes. Her seeing pieces had made her eye-whites red.

She complained that she couldn't keep them clean any longer. He knew nothing about such things. Leslie shivered and closed her wrap around her neck. "Chilly, isn't it?" she said.

"You are still weak." He threw fresh wood on the fire.

"Did you find out anything new?"

"A caravan came, but it was going to Wamba."

She looked at her timepiece. "What took you so long?"

"I had to return on a false path. I think there was a man from the police in Parsaloi."

"Police?"

"Yes, I believe so. He was not in uniform, but he acted like an official."

"There must be officials around who aren't from the police."

Firingin filled the teapot and placed it by the flames. "This is true, but the man said he was from Maralal, and he said it was peaceful there. That sounds like police trickery."

"Maybe the man left Maralal before the trouble started."

"That cannot be so. His clothes looked too fresh."

"Maybe things have changed there recently."

"Everybody, even the camel driver says the police and also the army have increased the searching. A driver said that the army now moves north of Maralal into the hills."

"The same ones we crossed?" she asked.

He nodded. "It may only be days before they come here," he said. "We must leave this place, soon. Tomorrow, I will go early to Parsaloi."

"Don't you think that official man will still be there?"

"Probably. But I must find a caravan. I cannot wait for him to leave."

He poured the tea. "That man did not notice me today," he added. "He talked loud but not to me. I left quickly."

"Maybe he's one who just likes to talk," Leslie said.

"Maybe."

After breakfast, the next morning, Firingin went to the town.

He waited at the central building less than an hour before a large caravan came in from the North. Four transients left with it. Only Firingin and two others continued waiting. One of the two was the man from Maralal.

After the caravan left, Firingin remained at the watering trough. He asked the boy cleaning up trash if more caravans were expected. The boy said that one usually came in from the South on this day of the week.

Firingin sat near the building to wait. The morning sun grew strong, and his eyelids drooped. He stood. He couldn't let himself fall asleep.

The time grew long, and Firingin considered going back to the camp. Leslie would be fearful after so many hours.

He was about to leave when he heard the sound of bawling camels. It came from the direction of the watering trough. He hurried to the front of the building and saw a line of beasts crowding for water. A caravan must have come in while he dozed. The other travelers were already standing around the animals.

The caravan drivers climbed over the backs of the camels, trying to prod them into an orderly queue. The work was difficult because the beasts remained loaded. They must have carried bags filled with water. The caravan would be going to the desert.

A large male camel kept two drivers occupied. One of the herders rode the animal, urging it away from the smaller females, and the other used a short pole to poke at the creature from the ground. With a loud roar, the male camel wheeled, knocking down the man with the pole.

The herder rolled away, but not fast enough to avoid the animal's kick. The driver coiled in obvious pain, and the enraged beast, now completely out of control, charged his downed adversary.

Seeing the danger, Firingin leaped the corner of the trough and ran toward the camel. He grabbed its chin-rope and hung on with both hands.

The beast tossed its head, but Firingin kept his grip.

In a frenzy, the animal swung its neck from side to side, but Firingin drug his heels until the swinging slowed. Then Firingin levered the huge head to the ground.

The driver on top dismounted and ran to his companion.

Firingin held the camel's nose against his leg and clucked a gentling sound in the animal's ear. Clucking often worked to calm restless cattle.

The male camel relaxed and gave up its anger.

Suddenly, a booming voice came from behind Firingin's back. "You know your camels," it said.

Firingin looked up and saw a large, bearded man above him. The man wore a turban that made him look like a king.

The man glared down waiting for his answer.

"I know beasts," Firingin said.

The beads on the man's turban rattled when he nodded toward the injured driver. "It appears I have need for one who knows beasts. Are you available for travel?"

"Where do you go?"

"We go to Korr. Northeast from here."

Firingin nodded. "I can go, but I have a woman. She must ride."

"We've already put on two passengers but bring her. We will leave as soon as these devils have had their fill."

22

The string of "wot, wots" from a low-hanging branch added an irritating monotony to Leslie's boredom. Today was the fifth day she'd been stuck in the camp by the river, but it seemed like forever. When she'd been so sick she hadn't noticed the surroundings; time didn't matter. Now, unfortunately, she was fully aware.

Firingin was away in the town and the jackal had lost interest in her, so she needed something to occupy her mind. If she just sat, her fears grew.

She searched through the bundle until she found the tablet and pencil. She wrote several pages in her journal. Much had happened since her last recording.

She included a long paragraph on the hazards of eating

leftover food in a hot climate.

A rustle from the bushes toward the river made her look up. She instinctively reached for the club but laid it back down when she saw Firingin. He looked hot and excited.

"Pack the things," he said. "We are leaving."

"Wonderful!" Leslie replied. "Where are we going? Not to Maralal, I suppose?"

"No. It is a caravan to Korr. But we must hurry. It will not wait."

She stuffed the tablet into the bag, and helped him gather up the blankets.

"Where is Korr?" she asked.

Firingin stuffed his robe into the bag and picked up the tattered container. "Hurry!" he said and urged her toward the opening in the thorn bushes.

He walked so fast Leslie couldn't keep up. Her feet were no longer sore, but one of her sandals needed a new strap.

"Slow down!" she said.

"We must hurry." He grabbed her hand and started pulling. She tripped and almost fell.

"Please, Leslie," he said. "The caravan will not wait."

"I can't."

He shook his head and lifted her to his shoulders.

When they approached the river, he told her to pull the wrap up over her face.

She looked through the slit and saw the town for the first time. Its low structures were the first buildings she had seen in nearly three weeks. It surprised her by its closeness to their camp. She wondered why she hadn't heard its noises. Perhaps there weren't many noises.

Spray splashed on her arms when Firingin waded into the shallow water. On the opposite side, he raced toward a line of low buildings.

He stopped at the corner of one building and lowered her to the ground. She peeked over the top of her wrap and saw a line of camels. They were tied together, noses to tails. Beside a large, brown creature at the front of the column, a giant man stood. He had a pointed beard and wore the robes of a potentate. His skin was black, but he looked more Arabian than African.

The man glared with humorless eyes.

"Make haste," he said in loud Swahili. "The animals grow restless."

"Which one should the woman ride?" Firingin asked.

The sultan—Leslie had dubbed the man on sight—pointed to a small, nearly white, camel in the middle of the chain.

Firingin lifted Leslie with the bundle to his shoulders. He walked toward the animal, and Leslie tried to arrange her legs.

"Isn't somebody going to tell me how to ride this creature?" she said.

"No time," Firingin said. The camel shied when they came close, and Firingin made a clucking sound in his throat. She laughed.

Without ceremony, Firingin placed her in the middle of the camel's back. The animal groaned and danced sideways when Leslie's weight settled between the two bags it already carried. She grabbed a crossbar on the bag carrier.

Firingin worked with poles that erected an awning over Leslie's head. "You only must hang on," he said. "The camel is tied to the others. It will not get lost."

"Quickly, driver!" the sultan bellowed.

The camel coughed, and the bags sloshed. "What's in these?" she asked.

"I must go to my post," Firingin said. He turned and ran toward the back of the train.

"Don't you have a camel?" she yelled after him. A jerk of the rope from the animal ahead, and Leslie grabbed with both hands. Her mount pitched itself into an ambling gait.

She peered around the edge of the awning and saw Firingin behind the caravan. He walked and waved his arms at the last camel in line.

The caravan headed up a small incline and onto a flat,

treeless plain. Dust came from the feet of the camels in front, and Leslie pulled the awning closed.

She could hear the sultan roaring orders from his throne on the brown giant. The drivers, one on each side and Firingin in the back, yelled and whistled at the animals.

Behind the sultan rode two other passengers. Both were men. The one, wrapped in a stained and faded blanket, appeared to be old. His head nodded with the motion of his camel; he was already asleep. The other man wore a cape like the one Firingin used to wear, except it was striped with bright colors. Under the cape, the man had on a tan shirt and shorts. She wondered if he was the one from Maralal.

Leslie was the only woman with the caravan. In her cocoon of filtered sunlight, it was easy for her to imagine herself being taken across the desert to join some sheik's harem—like an old Rudolph Valentino movie.

She opened the back of her shelter. She could barely see Firingin in the dust. His hair was coated white. She waved. He smiled and waved back.

Hours passed, and Leslie grew restless. She worked one of the blankets between her bottom and the camel's back. The hump of the creature made a poor fit with her posterior. Sitting on the makeshift perch had become painful, and the camel's rolling gait didn't help.

A musty smell rose from the animal or perhaps from the water bags. It had a pungency that gave Leslie a feeling of nausea.

She again opened the back of the awning. The desert air was dry. One whiff cleared away most of the odor, and her stomach settled.

The region the caravan was crossing continued to be dry and nearly treeless. Low bushes poked through soil that seemed to be a yellow-colored clay mixed with sand. They were definitely in a desert now. Leslie wished she could write some of the description in her diary. But even if she could have extracted the tablet from the bag, her hands were completely occupied by hanging on.

To pass time, she decided to sing. "I Been Workin' on the Railroad" seemed a good tune to keep time with the camel's motion.

She hadn't finished the first stanza when she felt a tug on her awning. She looked around and saw Firingin staring at her.

"Please," he said. "Do not sing in English."

She almost laughed when she saw the serious look on his face. The streaks of dust around his eyes made him look like a sad circus clown.

"Driver!" The sultan's shout made Firingin look away. "Get back to your position."

Firingin nodded his head once toward the well-dressed passenger and whispered, "He will hear." Then he ran to the rear.

She switched to the no problem song, but after three times through, she quit. It had begun to sound like the wot-wots of the hornbill.

The sun disappeared behind the western hills, and the caravan continued across the desert. Leslie could hear the mumbling of a conversation between the sultan and one of the male passengers. Occasionally the grunt of a camel invaded her enclosure.

The temperature cooled. As soon as it became dark, the clear sky let most of the day's heat escape. Leslie leaned back and gazed at the stars. She remembered the first night on Firingin's shoulders. She wished he would sing again.

One of the drivers on the side of the caravan began shouting, and Leslie's camel along with all the others started trotting. She gripped the crossbar.

"Keep them in line," the sultan roared. "They know our campsite."

Firingin ran toward the front of the column.

"Take the reins, you fools," the sultan commanded, "or all will be lost."

The camels were unloaded and hobbled for the night. A

large campfire lighted the fronts of the pitched tents. The travelers sat around the blaze and silently ate their meal.

Leslie picked at her food—only parts of it were palatable, the pita and the dates. Firingin and the others ate everything, even a mixture of yogurt and meat that looked mostly like floating grease.

After everyone had finished, the sultan assigned the job of cleaning up the dishes to Leslie. She almost gagged at the thought, but the man looked so fierce she had to obey.

Firingin gestured to remind her to keep her face covered.

One-handed, she eventually finished her task and rejoined the circle. The sultan had retired to his tent.

Leslie sat next to Firingin. The old passenger asked if anyone wanted to play bau. Nobody seemed interested.

One of the regular drivers pointed at Leslie and grinned. "In the desert, even one with great belief might drop her veil for a moment."

She pulled the cloth tighter. "She is also shy," Firingin said.

The other driver stood and stretched. "God will reward her," he said. He looked toward the sultan's tent. "But, the great one will have only condemnation for me if I do not take my post with the beasts." He turned and walked from the circle.

"Where do you go?" the remaining driver asked the old traveler.

"My people are near Ilaut," the old man said. "I will leave the caravan when we reach the other side of the Ndotos."

"Ilaut," the man from Maralal said. "I have never been there."

"It is a village of trading," the old man said. "The Rendille come there and so do people from the South."

"But the government has no station in Ilaut," the man from Maralal said.

"You are a government man?" the driver asked.

The man from Maralal nodded. "I go to Marsabit."

The circle grew quiet. Leslie wondered why. After a time, the driver rose to his feet and walked to the large tent near the sultan's. The old traveler had wrapped his blanket around his shoulders and closed his eyes.

The man from Maralal poked at the fire. Firingin watched him but said nothing. The man from Maralal left the circle. He seemed to be walking toward the camels, maybe to seek conversation with the driver on watch.

The light of a match showed his face in the distance, and the odor of cigarette smoke floated back.

Firingin leaned close to the old man's ear. "Do you know the family of Jeiso Hedaidile?" he asked.

She thought it strange that Firingin had suddenly been so outspoken.

The old traveler opened his eyes and looked curiously at Firingin. "No," he said. "But I have been in the South for many seasons."

Firingin opened his mouth as if to ask another question but quickly closed it. The man from Maralal had returned and stood watching in the shadows.

The circle again grew quiet. Firingin motioned for her to follow, and they went to the small tent that the sultan had assigned to them. The luxury of privacy had been afforded them because of Leslie. Even in an isolated desert camp, a woman was not allowed to sleep where her skin could be seen.

When they were alone, Leslie whispered, "I think you are right about that man. No one wanted to talk to him."

Firingin nodded. "He is not to be trusted."

"And where is this Marsabit he's going to?"

"It is beyond Korr. A government game reserve is there."

"Oh, well, a game warden won't bother us."

Firingin looked puzzled. She had used English in her sentence but couldn't think of a substitute.

"There is danger," he said. "I should not have asked the old one about my people."

"I wondered why you did that."

"I needed information, but the government man heard."

Leslie disrobed and crawled under the blankets.

"We must leave this caravan," Firingin said in a hushed voice.

"We can't. We're in the middle of nowhere."

"We must," he said. "When the old one leaves for Ilaut, we will also go."

"But you are one of the camel drivers. Won't the sultan be angry?"

He looked puzzled again. "The large man," she said. "Won't he be angry?"

"We cannot stay," Firingin said. "You cannot hide yourself forever."

"I don't think it's wise. Leaving will make the government man curious."

"It is possible," Firingin whispered, "But if we stayed, he would see your skin. He knows the name of my people. We could not escape."

The crackling sounds of the fire had faded. Soon it would be Firingin's turn for the watch. She pressed close to him. Her body was sore, but he felt good beside her.

23

Firingin sat inside the flap of the small tent and waited for Leslie to wiggle into her clothes. He raised his hand when she brushed against the canvas.

"Please," he whispered. "You must be quiet."

He held his ear next to the tent opening. No sounds came from the outside. The caravan drivers were sleeping soundly. Indeed, they would be tired after the previous day's march. At last evening's meal, the leader had said that they had made extraordinary progress. He'd told the old traveler that the caravan would arrive at the Ilaut crossing the following morning.

Firingin and Leslie would not wait for the crossing.

After the meal, he had made his preparations. He had packed their remaining goods into the bundle along with the portions of dates and pita, Leslie's favorite foods, he had saved from the evening's servings. Dates and pita would be all they would have to eat on the trek through the Ndotos Forest. He had tried to fix Leslie's sandal, but without leather, the repair he'd made would not last.

He would carry her most of the way.

"I'm ready," she whispered.

He nodded and crawled out of the tent. He felt himself shiver. The night air was cold in the desert.

Leslie emerged and started to speak. He held up his hand.

He directed her to follow him and hurried past the smoldering fire to the mound of stacked cargo carriers.

There they waited while the driver on sentry duty trudged to the far end of the circuit.

Crouching low, Firingin lead Leslie through the herd of hobbled camels. The huge male grunted and switched its tail but did not bolt.

When they reached the open desert, he signaled a halt. "We will go toward that star," he told her. He pointed at the bright one on the horizon. He could tell that she lacked confidence in his knowledge of this Ndotos country, so he told her of the star. Its direction was all he knew about their destination.

"The North Star," Leslie said. He lifted her to his shoulders and walked toward the open plain.

The sun had already risen above the low hills to the east, but Firingin and Leslie were nowhere near a forest.

Desert stretched in all directions. Its ground was covered with sharp rocks.

Firingin chose his steps carefully. A twisted ankle could mean death under the hot sun.

He stared toward a spot on the horizon. He'd thought earlier that he'd seen a scraggly tree there. It had vanished—perhaps it had been a mirage.

A slithery streak darted away from a large rock.

Firingin danced sideways. He stopped and waited. The reptile, a cobra, disappeared under a new shelter.

Leslie had not cried out. She must be asleep.

Another hour passed and still no trees. Firingin walked in silence. The temperature had climbed to a level higher than he had ever known.

He felt Leslie shift her weight.

"God, what a place!" she said. She'd used English, but her tone spoke the meaning.

"Keep yourself wrapped," he said. "The sun will burn."

"Can't we stop?"

He looked for a spot. Nearby, the parched ground was still covered with small rocks. It was not a place to camp. In the distance, a mountain sloped up from the plain. Dark areas suggested trees.

He pointed. "We will go there."

"That will take hours," she said. "I can't wait that long."

She had immediate needs and so did he. He kicked rocks aside and let her down.

After they relieved themselves, he reached to lift her back to his shoulders. She shook her head. "I'd rather walk."

It was too hot to argue. "Follow behind," he said.

He started toward the mountain, tramping the ground to scare away snakes.

The sun glared from above when Firingin, with Leslie on his shoulders again, reached a grassy area on the mountainside. A small acacia shaded a place where they could rest.

He lowered her to the ground and unpacked the blankets. A coucal bird sounded its call from a low branch. Its song made a welcome greeting.

"Am I thirsty!" Leslie said. She picked up the drinking bottle and carelessly pulled the cork. She drank large gulps, spilling water on her clothes.

"Slowly," he said.

"I'm sorry." She handed him the container. "You must be parched."

He waved it off. "I can wait, but do not waste."

They ate from the package of food, and after the meal, Leslie slept.

He dozed but tried to keep watch for predators. At sunset, he would wake her, and they would start again.

It must have been midnight when Firingin and Leslie reached the main trail to Ilaut. The thoroughfare was smooth, trampled by heavy foot traffic, and easily recognizable. He lowered her from his shoulders. She could now walk.

He removed his tattered sandals. On the pathway, he would travel barefoot.

In the nighttime coolness, they made their way easily, still following the direction of the bright star.

Only one party of fellow travelers met them. A man walked ahead of a woman who lead a donkey. They appeared to be Turkana so Firingin greeted them but said nothing more.

At morning's light, they came within view of a town.

Even though Firingin had never been to the region before, he recognized the village as Ilaut. Every Samburu had heard of the bald peak named Poi that stood on its outskirts.

He signaled a stop. Leslie did not need encouragement to rest. She leaned against his shoulder while he surveyed the scene before them.

From the nest of stick huts that surrounded Ilaut's central core came the barks of several dogs. Goats and a tethered herd of camels stirred the dust of the main street, but not a Land Rover or green-clad trooper was visible. Perhaps Leslie could rest in Ilaut without fear of discovery.

Firingin would talk to the owner of the tethered camels. If the caravan traveled north, he would offer his services as a driver.

The man feeding the camels seemed surprised by Firingin's question.

"Why do you want to go north?" he asked.

"I have family in the desert," Firingin replied.

"Well everyone to his own," the man said. "Which family is yours?"

"They are Rendille people."

"Everyone out there is Rendille or Turkana. What's the name?"

"Jeiso Hedaidile," Firingin answered. He hated to reveal his grandfather's name another time, but a driver taking them from this outpost would have to know the destination.

"Jeiso Hedaidile!" the man replied. A grin spread over his face. "Jeiso Hedaidile is the father of my own family."

Firingin said nothing. Such good fortune must not be disturbed by quick words. He looked at the man with renewed interest. This relative was not shaped like him. Short and round-faced, the man looked like a Kikuyu. Even his clothes looked strange. The wrap of bright cloth around his head made him look like a trader from Somalia.

"Where do you come from?" the man said.

"I am from the South. Near Maralal. My mother is Jeiso's daughter."

"The one who married the Samburu. I remember hearing about her."

Firingin nodded.

"My father, Hedadam, is Jeiso's son," the man said. "Not his only son. Half the people between here and Kargi are in Jeiso's family. My name is Hedad."

The man extended his hand.

Firingin held back the traditional Samburu greeting. Not all people were honored by the spitting. He gave his name and pumped the hand of the man named Hedad.

"I'd be happy to take you north, cousin Firingin," Hedad said.

"I have a woman with me," Firingin said. "She will need to ride."

"And where is this woman?"

"She sleeps in the shade near the store. I must return to her and tell of our good fortune."

"Tell her it will be a long trip. We go to South Horr first. I have fourteen camels loaded with salt and millet. Does your woman ride well?"

"She has ridden, but she is not used to the desert. The woman is a thin-skin."

"A what?"

"A white woman," Firingin replied. Even the sister named thin-skins that way.

"What are you doing with a white woman? She's not your wife, is she?"

"She is not my wife. She is not even my woman, but she shows great liking for me."

Hedad held up his hand. "Bring her here at sunset, and we will take her to see old Jeiso. I hope she can sleep while she rides. We will not camp at night—the practice is unwise in the land of the Turkana."

"I have skills with the beasts," Firingin said. "I can help with driving your camels."

"That's excellent!" Hedad said. "I'm sure to be short-handed. My drivers forget their caravan duties when they smell the women of this town."

Firingin smiled. Already Cousin Hedad talked to him as an equal.

Leslie wasn't asleep when Firingin returned to her. A crowd of children had collected around the place where she rested.

Firingin settled to sit beside her. She was drawing images of her homeland for the young ones. In the past, she had shown Firingin drawings of America, but he would gladly watch again. The wheeled vehicles, flying machines, and dwellings she portrayed were like magic things. Structures in her land had many levels and towered high above her drawings of Samburu dwellings.

Leslie talked to the children, using a mixture of Swahili and English. She filled all of her papers with drawings, giving the completed sheets to the children.

When she had no more, the young ones clamored and pulled at her arms. She looked sad and shook her head.

The children with filled sheets ran away, and the others chased them.

"I need a new tablet," Leslie said. "Have you any money?"

"I have jewelry. We can trade it."

Few items were on the shelves of the Ilaut store. Like everything in the town, it was far from commercial Kenya. Leslie went from aisle to aisle, looking for the paper, and Firingin looked for replacement sandals. In a back corner, Leslie found a stack of tablets and some pencils. She purchased them all, and Firingin bought a needle and some leather string.

"I have found a caravan," he said, when they left the store. "It leaves tonight for the desert."

"I hope it has a better leader than the last one," she said. She would not forgive the large one for making her clean up after meals.

"Its leader is my relative," Firingin replied. "He will take us to the village of my grandfather."

"You're not serious!" she said.

He smiled and nodded. The row of camels stood in front of the low buildings.

With Firingin's help, Hedad and two of his drivers hitched the animals, one by one, into a train.

When all was ready, Hedad walked to a nearby alley and stared at the community of huts.

He returned and looked at Firingin. "They are not coming. Let's put the woman on the old female in front. A she-camel will give the easiest ride."

Hedad commanded the animal to kneel, but Firingin shook his head. "The woman does not know how to mount."

Hedad smiled and tapped the camel's neck. The creature stood, and Firingin lifted Leslie to its back.

Hedad shrugged and looked once more toward the street. He turned back and waved Firingin and the other drivers to their positions. A loud whistle issued from Firingin's cousin, and the line of camels lurched to life.

A cloud of dust rose behind the beasts. Firingin smiled because he would not have to breathe kicked-up sand on this trip. Hedad had placed him in the favored post on the windward side of the column.

Firingin waved at Leslie. It would be a long ride for her. Maybe, when it was over, she could sleep.

24

Leslie rode comfortably on the gentle-gaited camel. Before her stretched dry rolling hills and the golden sky of an African sunset. Below her camel's reaching neck, walked the short man who was Firingin's cousin. He didn't seem like Firingin at all. He laughed often and talked with twinkling eyes. The man named Hedad was so short and carefree-seeming and Firingin was so tall and solemn it was difficult to believe they were related in any way.

Firingin walked to one side of the caravan. He was as happy as she'd seen him. Once she even heard him singing.

Except for midday when the sun glared with blast-furnace intensity, Leslie rode with her face uncovered.

She wondered how her face looked after all her days in the

open. She'd tried to see her reflection in a pool of water in Ilaut, but she couldn't really tell how dark her countenance had become. Her hands and arms were deep brown.

She'd given up on the contacts. Her attempts at salt solutions for cleaning had been dismal failures. Eventually her eyes got so sore she had to abandon the lenses. At least it didn't effect her seeing of the important things in her current existence, things far away and writing or pictures on the tablet.

Sometimes from her podium atop the rolling camel, she sang. Nobody cared in this caravan. Hedad often looked up at her, and after he'd watched for a stanza or two would join in. He didn't know English, but he would wail through the repetitive parts in a wheezy-sounding voice. The first time, she almost busted out laughing.

The caravan rarely stopped. When it did, the first order of business was for everyone to go to the toilet. All of the drivers discreetly turned their backs while Leslie did her business.

Near noon on the second day, according to Leslie's still-operating watch, they stopped at a brackish watering hole. The camels didn't need water, Hedad said, but they were allowed to drink anyhow. It made quite a sight to see them side by side, craning their necks down toward the small pool. Camels looked like romantic animals, but their natures were anything but agreeable. They never received any command from a driver without complaint. Firingin had about the best way with them. He seemed to do well with animals.

Food and water were consumed by the drivers while they walked. Each had a pouch of dates at his waist and a bottle of water under his arm. Leslie also had provisions and ate without leaving her mount. The motion of her camel was easy. Sometimes she even slept.

Near sunset on the second day, the caravan approached a range of high mountains. Firingin ran alongside Leslie's camel and pointed to the tallest peak.

"The mountain is Ng'iro," he said. "It is a sacred place to all Samburus."

"Sacred? In what way?"

"It is the home of Nkai."

"Nkai? Is that your word for God?"

He obviously hadn't understood the question. "I have not seen the home of the Holy one before this day," he said. "I am greatly honored."

She nodded. In spite of the weeks they had spent together, he could still surprise her.

The caravan camped outside a village at the base of the mountains. Hedad said the village was South Horr. They would enter it the next morning when he would be able to complete his trading.

Everyone was silent around the campfire. One of the drivers cooked some grain and made tea. Leslie ate a few bites and immediately felt sleepy. She asked Firingin to find the blankets. Near the fire, she stretched out and fell into a sleep fed by total exhaustion.

When the caravan entered the village, Leslie saw that South Horr was a bigger town than either Parsaloi or Ilaut. Even a few dusty automobiles and Land Rovers sat along its streets.

Firingin looked nervous and, before they reached the main area, reminded her to cover her face. He didn't go with Hedad to the market but stayed near the camels, almost hiding inside the circle of tethered animals.

She saw a store a distance down the street. "I think I'll go there," she said. "They might have sandals for sale."

Firingin shook his head. "Do not go."

"I can trade my watch," she said, "and I need sandals."

"This town could have police," he said.

"All the better. If there's a police station, I could turn myself in. It would solve your problem of returning me, just like that."

Firingin stared at her. He said nothing at first, and then he looked sad. "You are no problem to me, Leslie," he said.

He continued to look at her. It was the first time his eyes

had shown real affection to her.

She hadn't kissed him since the night on the river, but suddenly she needed to. She checked to see if anyone was watching. The other drivers were occupied with a board game, so she raised up on her toes and pressed her lips to his.

He looked surprised and quickly wiped his mouth.

Then he laughed, and she laughed too.

25

On the evening of the third day after leaving South Horr, the camels of the caravan all started bawling at once. They started to pick up their pace, and Hedad ordered the drivers to close in. Soon the dwellings of a village came into view. It was Jeiso's village.

Firingin knew because Hedad had told him at the stop for water that they would arrive before sunset.

"Hold the ropes," Hedad shouted. The camels had started running, and Leslie leaned forward in her perch atop the lead female.

The caravan passed near several dwellings, and Firingin saw smoke rising above the skin-covered roofs. The evening meals were being prepared.

To the west of the village, a line of low hills broke the flat plain and held the smoke in a cloud of still air. It was a scene that reminded him of his home manyatta.

Firingin had grabbed a line between two camels near the middle of the train. He pulled back as hard as he could but couldn't seem to slow the charge. It continued past the village and directly toward the barricaded corral on the other side. All of the drivers strained on the ropes, but the animals kept running.

Firingin moved toward the lead camel. At least he would get Leslie off her runaway mount. He reached for her, and just as he did, the lead camel and her followers suddenly braked to shuffling halt.

As though nothing unusual had happened, Hedad walked back from the front of the train.

"Take the woman down," he said to Firingin. "After we unload the beasts, I will show you to Jeiso."

In the past, Firingin hadn't formed any opinion of his mother's father. He'd been told that the man was old; Jeiso Hedaidile was said to be one of the oldest patriarchs in the desert country. Firingin knew little else. He'd never heard if his grandfather was stern like the father or if he was happy like Hedad. Firingin did not believe he would be like Hedad. He'd never seen a headman who was as happy as his cousin.

Hedad took Leslie and Firingin straight through the center of the village. They passed groups of elderly men who sat near the doorways of dwellings. The men smiled and waved. Several pointed to Leslie and started talking rapidly.

Could they tell that she was a thin-skin? She had her face covered. It was the first time since leaving South Horr that she'd needed secrecy.

"That's him," Hedad said. He pointed at a wrinkled old one who sat on his haunches playing bau.

"Jeiso!" Hedad said, using a loud voice. "I have brought visitors."

The old man looked at Hedad and smiled a nearly toothless

smile. "Hedad, my grandson. Welcome home."

Hedad gestured toward Firingin. "This is the son of your daughter. The one who lives with the Samburus. His name is Firingin."

The old man laughed. He laughed until water ran from his eyes and he had to cough for breath. After a few minutes, he controlled the spasms. "The Samburu was a fool," he said and laughed again.

Hedad looked embarrassed. "I have not seen him like this before," he said.

Firingin would have asked why Jeiso laughed, but he wasn't sure he wanted hear the answer. His Samburu disgrace must have spread all the way to the old one's ears.

Jeiso stopped laughing and stared at Leslie.

"This is a woman that Firingin has brought to see you," Hedad said. "She is a white woman."

Jeiso rose to his feet and took a halting step in Leslie's direction. His legs became unsteady, and he stopped. He beckoned to her.

"Come close," he said in Swahili.

She looked at Firingin. He nodded. It would have been impolite for her to stay back.

She obeyed the summons, and when she got within his reach, Jeiso pulled away her wrap.

He grinned without shame at her exposed body. "She is not white," he said. "Her skin is pink."

Hedad whispered to Firingin, "I don't believe Jeiso has seen a white woman before."

Leslie redid her wrap, and the old man took her by the arm. "Come," he said. "You will eat in my lodge tonight."

Leslie pulled back and grabbed Firingin's hand.

Jeiso turned toward him. "Come, Honored Grandson," he said. "You must join your pink woman at my fire."

Honored Grandson! Firingin followed but was puzzled. If Jeiso acknowledged him so, why had he laughed?

As they ate the meal, Jeiso asked Firingin about his mother

and about the sister. The old man recited from messages he had received from the sister about Firingin.

Jeiso said he was proud that one of his own had become such an educated man.

The dwelling was small and crowded with Jeiso's wives. They did not speak, but served dishes of heated camel's milk, lamb's meat, and dates. Leslie sat beside Jeiso and chose small pieces of the food while she fought off the old one's inquisitive touches of her body. She seemed angry and slapped at Jeiso's hands, but she did not deter him.

Firingin did not make so bold as to object. He had seen such curiosity from old men. Before the meal was completed, the ancient fingers would rest from their examination of the pink body.

After the eating, Jeiso smoked. Firingin showed him his knife. Jeiso turned the weapon over in his hand, and his eyes glistened.

"You are young to be honored with a headsman's knife," Jeiso said. He handed the weapon back to Firingin. "You must be a great man among the Samburu."

Firingin had no idea what to say. Jeiso must be making jokes.

Jeiso told Leslie and Firingin that they would sleep in his lodge. In the morning, he would direct his wives to construct a dwelling for his guests. The old one did not ask why they had come or how long they would stay in his village. If he had asked of the duration, Firingin would have answered that it would not be long. Leslie would soon tire of this life—the food which she did not like, the hot dusty surroundings and smells of animals, the vermin, insects and reptiles that lived in the desert, and most of all the curiosity of Jeiso. It would be a short time before she would want to return, perhaps to South Horr. But, it was not a time that Firingin wished for.

Indeed, he had become accustomed to Leslie. Not just the sex. He also liked other things, like her interest in the young ones and her willingness to explain things to them and to him.

He would miss her because of those things, but mostly he would miss her affection for him.

Two days later, Firingin and Leslie moved into the new dwelling. It was close to Jeiso's lodge and yet distant enough for Leslie to feel courage for sex. Her bleeding season was over, and her hunger for him seemed greater than ever. He entered her four times. She was as energetic as before, but he was glad she had learned to control her screaming.

Firingin and Leslie had spent nearly a day in their dwelling before Firingin gave it the customary new owner's inspection. Never had he seen a living space that was so well furnished. New blankets and camel-skin robes adorned the sleeping area; new cooking and serving utensils, most made of metal, hung along the wall beside the fire pit; and a fuel-burning lantern sat in a place of honor at the back of the room.

Leslie did not seem impressed. As soon as she woke up from her resting after sex, she went outside. She told him that she wanted to watch the people. Leslie's curiosity about people was also a thing that he liked.

A few men and many women and children crowded around to see her. Some tried to pull back her clothing, but she quickly pushed them away. Several women talked to her in Swahili, and one spoke words in English. That noon the woman who spoke English brought food to their dwelling. Leslie talked with the woman all afternoon.

Firingin became bored with their talk and went outside. He went to the corral. It would be interesting to see how the Rendille tended their animals.

He soon discovered that the village herders worked close to the corral. Grazing in the desert was sparse, so much of the feeding was done using fodder brought from the South by the village's caravans.

The herds were mixed, mostly camels but also a few cattle and a number of goats and sheep. In the dry season, he was told, distant excursions were made to find watering holes. When grazing increased after rains, some of the cattle and sheep were taken to the nearby hills.

Firingin had never been one for conversation and found it difficult to talk at length with the young herders. They did not speak good Swahili and the tribal dialect they used was hard to comprehend. He left the corral area and drifted back to the cluster of dwellings.

He looked for Hedad, but the caravan leader was nowhere to be seen. When Firingin interrupted Jeiso's game to ask about his cousin, the old one simply growled that Hedad was with his woman.

Days went by, and Leslie and the woman who spoke English became good friends. Other women also gathered around Leslie, and Firingin was pleased when they started teaching her skills for keeping up the house.

In time, Leslie's popularity became a concern to him. Instead of growing tired of the village, she seemed to have become one of its most important inhabitants.

After a week, their dwelling filled every morning with the village's children. Leslie had started a school for teaching language and numbers to the young ones.

The mothers of the students paid for her services by bringing daily food and water as well as fuel for the fireplace. The needs of the household were provided through Leslie's school, and Firingin began to feel useless. As Jeiso's guest, he was not allowed to assume duties around the village. He was supposed to have all the time he needed for conversations with friends and relatives.

He did not, however, find the freedom of Jeiso's village to be satisfying. In the daytime hours, he stayed around the gaming area by Jeiso's dwelling and tried to talk with some of the old ones. Soon they started repeating their stories, and Firingin yearned for other conversations.

Hedad came twice to the place where games were played. Both of the times he appeared, his wife quickly came and took him away. It was said that Hedad was never free of his woman when he was in the village. They had no children. Rendilles without children have low status, so Hedad's wife kept him on the blankets. Hedad seemed happier with the caravan than he did at home.

After conversation with the elder ones completely ran out, Firingin was reduced to silently watching endless hours of bau. He tried playing a few times, but soon lost interest.

One morning as he stood observing Jeiso beat his second opponent of the day, Firingin felt a tap on his shoulder. He turned and saw Hedad.

"I have come to say good-bye," Hedad said. "I start tonight for Kargi."

Firingin shook his cousin's hand. They hadn't spent much time together in the village, but Firingin would certainly miss him.

"How long will you be gone?"

"Two weeks, maybe three. After Kargi we will go to Ilaut and then South Horr. They're my usual stops."

"I will probably be here when you return," Firingin said. "The woman seems happy teaching the children."

"Yes. My neighbors' children go to her. I am told they learn many things."

"I cannot even stay in the dwelling," Firingin said.

Hedad's face opened in a grin. "Why don't you come with my caravan?" he said. "I could use an extra driver. We take a herd of yearlings to market in Kargi. A herder with your skill would be a big help."

"I would, except for the woman. She would grow sad, being alone so far from her people."

"It seems to me she is less alone than you, my friend."

Firingin nodded. It was true. He was the one who had grown unhappy.

"She won't mind if you go," Hedad added. "Ask her."

Firingin did not like the suggestion. It was not the way of a Samburu to ask for a woman's permission.

"I will tell her," he said. "When does your caravan leave?"

"As usual, at sunset."

"I will be there."

A familiar scene greeted Firingin when he ducked through the doorway of the dwelling. Leslie sat with a stack of paper and drew pictures for a circle of children. Voices were loud and excited as the children competed to give answers to her questions.

"Leslie," he said. "I have something to tell you."

She looked startled and put down the paper. Since she had thrown away her seeing pieces, she did not always notice things.

All eyes of the children turned toward him. "Wait, please," she said to the circle.

She came to Firingin. Her face looked frightened.

"What is it?" she said.

"I am going with Hedad's caravan."

She said nothing. He could see that she was thinking of a response.

"How long would you be gone?" she finally asked.

"Maybe three weeks. He goes to Ilaut and South Horr. He has a herd of yearlings to sell."

She turned and looked at the children then back to him. Her eyes looked moist. "When would you go?"

"I will go tonight," he answered. He would not bargain with her.

"And your mind is made up?" she said. He didn't completely understand her sentence so didn't answer.

She walked back to the circle. "I need more paper," she said, "and bring me pencils and..." She spoke to one of the children, and the child relayed her message.

"Teacher wants you to bring her coloring pencils," the boy said.

He nodded. His eyes sought Leslie's. "Can I be with you before I go?"

"No!" she said. "Just go!"

He felt bad but would not be weak and change his mind.

26

Leslie stared at the line of camels until they disappeared in the evening mist. Hedad's whistles and shouts still rang in her ears, but the empty feeling had already started.

She knew Firingin had become restless, but why did he have to leave her? Jeiso's people were his family; it wasn't her fault he couldn't be happy with them. He was too solitary—even among his own.

She went to the back of the dwelling and lit the lantern. She wrote an account of the day in her diary, but it didn't quell her sense of dread. How would she make it through the nights without him? Until he left, she hadn't realized how much she depended on him for protection. Thoughts of nocturnal creatures creeping, unchecked by his presence, into her blankets brought a dryness to her mouth. She had seen the numbers of reptile and animal carcasses brought in by the men of the village. The region must be swarming with vermin.

She tried to reason away her fears. Her dwelling was near the center of the community. Many people would be sleeping between her and the open desert.

Her days wouldn't be bad. The school was going great. Only one or two of the young children of the village did not attend. Even most of the girls were now coming. She was actually collecting so much food from the mothers that she had started a lunch program for the students. A couple of the women helped each day with the preparation and serving.

Old Jeiso had come around several days ago to heap praises on her. Luckily he'd behaved himself. It was the first time that she'd been within reach of him since that first uncomfortable night.

Leslie went to the bundle of things left from the trip and found the club Firingin had cut for her. She leaned it against the wall near the sleeping area. If every so often she beat on the floor, she might scare away any potential intruders. Perhaps she could survive that way until Firingin returned.

Outside her hut, the village grew quiet. The women and girls had come in from the corral with the jugs of evening milk, and the herders were bedding down the animals.

Leslie hadn't drunk any fresh camel's milk, but she had tried some of the yogurt. When everyone else eats something, you have to eventually give in. After the first spoonful, it hadn't been so bad.

She rummaged through the food containers around her fireplace. She wasn't particularly hungry but felt she should eat. Maintaining a mealtime routine would be an important part of keeping her life together.

Most of the containers were empty. She had thrown out the boiled rice—one of the women had said it smelled tainted. That was all Leslie had needed to get rid of it.

She grabbed a handful of dates and crawled to the fresher

air of the doorway.

A glowing sliver of moon followed the sun toward the ridge of western hills. The sky above had already turned from the red of evening to the star-filled purple of night. Seeing the Milky Way, Leslie thought of her first night on Firingin's shoulders. It seemed like years had passed since that wonderful ride.

Only a few people remained in the courtyard. Across the open area, Leslie saw her English-speaking friend, Wambila. The woman was coaxing her children into her dwelling.

Wambila looked up and waved. "Leslie," she yelled, "come eat with us."

Wambila was one of the mothers who had served that day. She probably knew that the children had eaten all that was good of Leslie's food.

Leslie quickly accepted. She had eaten with Wambila before, and her friend served the kind of dishes she liked. Besides, Leslie simply enjoyed keeping company with the statuesque woman. Wambila had taught her much about living among the Rendille.

Wambila's English was incredible considering that she had not learned it through formal schooling. She'd apparently acquired her skill through repeated use of the words her husband had brought back from his trading expeditions.

Wambila told Leslie that before Hedad, her husband had been the senior caravan leader of Jeiso's family. He had traveled for many years to towns and villages of the region—some as far away as Marsabit and Maralal. After an injury from a rampaging camel, he sat and played games with Jeiso and the elders.

Leslie thought Wambila was the most beautiful of the women in the village. Her nearly six-foot height was emphasized by the luxurious cockscomb hairdo she always wore. She had told Leslie that the hairdo was a symbol of her status as mother of a principal heir to the family's wealth. Wambila seemed young to be an honored mother. The ravages of a desert life had not taken the smoothness from her skin or dulled the enthusiastic look in her eyes. She was obviously one who was still had an interest in adventure.

"How does it feel to be left alone?" Wambila said after Leslie settled beside the fireplace.

"I will miss him. But it is true. He was bored in the village."

Wambila served Leslie from a platter of roast lamb.

"We all saw him hanging around, looking forlorn," she said. "Not much of a talker, is he?"

"He has other ways of expressing himself."

Wambila smiled. "I'll bet he does."

"I will miss him most at night. I felt so safe with him there. Now..."

"Don't worry. I was told that Jeiso has assigned a watch of warriors to patrol around your dwelling. Nothing will intrude on your sleep."

Leslie beamed. The old man constantly amazed her.

She winked at Wambila. "I wonder if the patrol will also guard me from the hands of Jeiso."

Wambila swatted one of her young ones away from a second helping. She glared down the defiant boy and turned her gaze back to Leslie. "The old man is harmless," she said. "He has fathered many in his day but now only dreams of conquests."

"I don't know. The first night Firingin and I were here, I thought Jeiso would take me right at the sitting for dinner. Poor Firingin, he looked so uncomfortable."

"Firingin is too much of a Samburu," Wambila said. "He lets pride rule his thoughts."

"You notice that, too."

"Hedad will change him. You'll see. Firingin will come back from this trip acting like a Rendille."

Leslie smiled. Wambila sounded like she expected them to be staying in the village. It wouldn't be bad, especially if Firingin were happy. Maybe someday they would even get married. She shook her head. It was too much to hope for.

The days after Firingin's departure became weeks, but Leslie stayed busy with her school. The children progressed rapidly. Some were even starting addition and subtraction.

She had grown accustomed to the crunch of footsteps around her dwelling at night. She rarely saw the warriors. They took their posts unobtrusively after each sunset and were always gone when she came out of her doorway in the morning.

She risked a visit to Jeiso to thank him for the protection. He was gracious, even offering her a puff on his water-pipe. Jeiso's three wives hovered in the back of the dwelling. They had never been friendly. They might have harbored a jealousy toward her, but no one had said so.

One morning early in the third week, Leslie awoke with a sickness in her stomach. She thought it was the cooked millet she had eaten the night before, a leftover like the infamous rice. She wouldn't eat it again.

She vomited but continued feeling nauseous. She decided to cancel school. If it was a virus, she didn't want to spread it to the children. She'd heard enough about the way the whites had spread killer diseases to native people in America.

The following morning she was nauseous again. She wondered if it might be something else. Her period was at least a week late.

Another week had passed and still no sign of a period. She was still nauseous every morning, but she'd resumed classes. It was almost certain now that she was pregnant. She'd begun to wonder if the village had such a thing as a visiting doctor.

"But you and Firingin aren't married," Wambila said after Leslie told her and asked about medical treatment.

"No. But we care a great deal for each other."

"Tribal tradition will not allow it," Wambila said.

"Allow what?"

"You to have the baby."

"But it's ours, not the tribe's."

"In Rendille villages, Leslie, food is often scarce. Since

you've been here, there's been plenty, but the drought or an unsuccessful trading expedition can suddenly make life difficult. The number of children born into the tribe must be controlled. A baby of an unmarried woman is considered an unacceptable burden."

"What if Firingin and I do get married?"

"It would be different then, but he is not here. How can you be sure he can afford to marry, or that he will want to accept the responsibility."

"Responsibility is his middle name. He'll accept responsibility."

Wambila looked sadly at Leslie. "I will keep your secret for a while," she said, "but Firingin had better come home soon."

"If he doesn't?"

"Jeiso will have to be told."

Leslie could feel herself growing testy. "And?" she fired back.

"Usually the pregnancy is aborted immediately."

"God!"

"It's not that bad," Wambila said. "We do it with herbs and heavy food in most cases."

Leslie left Wambila's dwelling feeling angry but also terrified. Each glance as she walked across the courtyard worried her. Would the curious Rendilles discover her condition before Firingin came back?

In the days that followed, she tried to avoid Jeiso and especially his wives. But she worried that avoiding them would also cause suspicion. She was torn between the need to keep her condition hidden and the need to act normal. She continued her school, but lived in terror that one of the students or a mother would notice a thickening of her midriff. And she wondered in her paranoia, if one of Jeiso's glances at her body could bring discovery and death to her unborn baby?

When it left for Kargi, Hedad's caravan went directly into the heart of the Chalbi Desert. Each day the procession traveled, it crossed through basins of chalky alkaline under a sky filled with glaring light and towering dust funnels.

A smudge in the vastness, the line of fourteen camels with the herd of five yearlings behind, tracked across open plains and through stands of dried vegetation. Everywhere, wire-hard balls of thorns rolled in the hot wind.

A four-day run to market without a camp would stretch the camels and the yearlings to their limits, but Hedad would not allow an overnight stop. He said the sooner the wild, young camels were delivered, the better it would be for everyone.

The yearlings were being handled by a veteran camel

driver named Keigo. The three boys who helped him were getting their first exposure to caravan life.

Hedad and Firingin held responsibility for the adult camels. Using continuous fore and aft patrols, the two cousins kept the line of stately beasts at a steady walk ahead of Keigo's unruly mob.

On this first leg of the expedition, the caravan carried only light cargo, fodder for the camels, and provisions for the drivers. In Kargi, the yearlings would be sold and springwater along with perhaps some salt would be purchased for transport to Ilaut. There it would be traded for grain and southern-grown fodder.

Alone on one side of the line, Firingin had to keep running to keep each animal in its place. His legs grew tired, but he didn't mind. It felt good to be useful again.

He thought of Leslie and wondered how she would get along by herself. He knew she would be afraid at night.

To protect her from what she feared, he'd stopped at the gaming area before he left and asked Jeiso to provide guards for her dwelling. Without hesitation, the old one had pledged the full coverage of his warriors.

How different Jeiso was from the father. Generous and good natured, the Rendille patriarch seemed to actually enjoy serving his family.

The expedition arrived in Kargi a day early, but Hedad's face showed unhappiness. As soon as the camels had been kneeled on the village's main street, he walked to one of the low buildings.

"Is there a problem?" Firingin asked Keigo.

"Didn't you see?" the grizzled driver asked. "The camel market has been abandoned. We have brought these wild ones for nothing."

When Hedad returned, he said, "It's been moved to Korr, almost a week's drive from here."

The boys groaned, but no one paid attention.

"How about the town springs?" Keigo asked.

"No extra water. That's why the market was moved."

Firingin surveyed the street to see if anyone looked like a police officer. The town of Kargi appeared peaceful, but he couldn't be sure such an unfamiliar place would remain that way. He'd be relieved when the caravan was again on the move.

"Tomorrow a trader comes in from Ethiopia," Hedad said. "We'll need to buy fodder from him for our trip to Korr." He turned to Keigo. "You and the boys water the yearlings and corral them near the riverbed south of the village. Firingin and I will stay until the trader arrives. We will meet you by the river when the caravan is ready to travel."

One of the yearlings levered itself to its feet and stumbled against its hobbles. Two of the boys ran to kneel the animal. The third boy dozed beside a building.

Keigo turned his back toward the sleeping boy and spoke softly to Hedad. "Jeido grows weary of the drive. I will need more herders for the trip to Korr."

"Yes," Hedad replied. "I will see to it."

Uncomfortable in the town, Firingin busied himself with the adult camels and tried to appear inconspicuous.

He soon learned, however, that he could not hide from the people of Kargi. The more he tried to assume the role of a preoccupied camel driver, the more passersby stopped to ask questions. They wanted to know who he was and where he was from. While he avoided giving answers, he had to agree that the people of the town had a right to be curious. Without his jewelry there was nothing to show which tribe he was from, and tribal affiliation was an important thing to know about a newcomer. Through the day, he spoke as little as possible. He feared his dialect might give away his Samburu origins and generate even more curiosity.

Hedad was gone most of the day, presumably recruiting new drivers. When he returned to the caravan in the late afternoon, Firingin suggested to him that the camels be moved to the edge of town. The fodder was nearly gone. Firingin had seen a small patch of dry grass on the outskirts when they'd arrived.

Hedad sanctioned the move, but only if Firingin would consent to stay in the desert with the beasts. He actually seemed surprised by Firingin's enthusiastic affirmative. Hedad did not know of Firingin's need for secrecy.

That night, Firingin slept in the open desert, away from the probing questioners of Kargi. The flanks of the gentle she-camel made him a pillow, and only the rumblings of her digestive chambers disturbed his peace.

In the morning, Hedad approached Firingin's outpost with two men in tow.

"These are our new drivers," he said. "They will help you bring the caravan to the market place. The salt trader from the North has arrived, and I must now go and bargain with him."

Firingin and the drivers brought the camels to the center of town and waited while Hedad bought all the extra fodder that the Ethiopian had. From the street, Firingin could hear his cousin arguing with the sharp-eyed trader over every shilling of the price. It was easy to see why Hedad was Jeiso's main caravan leader.

They quickly loaded the bags of Hedad's purchase on the adult camels and left for the riverbed. Hedad scouted ahead, making marks in the soil, and Firingin followed with the train of animals.

All afternoon, they searched the sandy tributaries but found no sign of the yearlings. "Those fools have lost themselves," Hedad said, when he returned at sunset.

"We'll have to camp and look more in the morning. I don't understand Keigo being careless this way."

That night around the campfire, the new drivers talked.

"A trader from Korr stopped in town last week," one of them said. "He told of a crazy man who is being hunted in the South."

"Crazy man?" Hedad said.

"Yes! They say a Samburu went wild and killed an armed

soldier," the other replied.

Firingin stared into the fire and said nothing.

"A Samburu killing a soldier!" Hedad said. "That would be crazy. Where did it happen?"

"Maralal," the man said. "The soldier was there to search for the white woman."

"White woman?" Hedad said. He looked across the flames at Firingin.

"Haven't you heard about the white woman?" the driver said.

"No!" Hedad said. "I've heard nothing." Firingin saw Hedad's jaw tighten.

"I thought everyone knew of the one who was stolen from the tourists," the man said.

"We have been in the desert for several weeks," Hedad replied. "Far from such stories."

"People say that the police have been searching for over a month," the driver said. "It is said that the killer and the woman have completely vanished."

The circle grew silent. Nothing but the crackle of the fire disturbed the stillness.

Hedad stood and stretched his arms. "This talk of Samburus and white women is interesting," he said, "but I have beasts to check."

"But what we say is true," the driver said. "Everyone from the South talks of it."

Hedad was short in height with short arms and legs, but he gained stature from his manner. "Nothing but stories," he said directly to the driver. "You have told us gossip. In these times, white women do not get stolen by the Samburu or anybody else. You have passed on rumors made up by old men who are bored with their lives."

The driver shrugged. "Everyone talks of it." The drivers tried to say more, but Firingin made loud noises while cleaning the bowls from the meal. The drivers grew discouraged and retired to their bedrolls.

When Hedad came back from the animals, Firingin sat by the fire.

"It's you, isn't it?" Hedad whispered.

Firingin nodded. "The soldier would have killed me."

"But why did you take the woman?"

"I didn't. I was trying to return her. I brought her to Jeiso's village hoping the police would stop looking."

"Well, that apparently hasn't happened," Hedad said. He looked toward the snoring drivers and back to Firingin. "What will you do now?"

"I do not know." Firingin gazed at the fire.

"Have you told Jeiso?"

"Not yet," Firingin said. "When we return, I will. Then I will take the woman back."

Hedad gave a final poke to the embers. He rose to his feet and clapped a hand on Firingin's shoulder.

"Time to sleep, my friend."

The following morning they found the yearling herd in a narrow canyon away from the river. Keigo explained that the boys had grown restless while guarding the animals. He had chosen the ravine as a natural corral.

Hedad gave Keigo a damning look. After assigning one of the new drivers to help with the yearlings, he ordered Keigo to bring his charges from the canyon. The expedition started immediately for Korr.

Five days later, Hedad's ragged collection of men and camels arrived on the outskirts of the sprawling town. Hedad had grown somber, and Firingin pondered the reasons. It might have been his cousin's concern about having a fugitive in his group, but Hedad had spoken several times of the expedition's other troubles. A day after it had left Kargi, a yearling had been bitten by an adder and had died. The loss of that animal plus the general decline of the others had reduced Hedad's expected profits to nearly zero. He lamented over the dismal report he would have to make to Jeiso.

When the caravan passed the first scattering of Korr's

outlying dwellings, Firingin walked to a position beside Hedad.

"I should not go into this town," Firingin said. "It is a large settlement. The police can be here."

"Yes, I know," Hedad said. "You must wait outside." He swung his arm to one side. "Stay in this area. We will come back this way."

When the caravan passed the next cluster of dome-shaped huts, Firingin dropped away from his post. By the time he'd found shade beside one of the structures, the line camels and its following herd of young animals had become a blur against the dancing light.

Firingin watched the children who played nearby.

They reminded him of the students in Leslie's school. He thought of how he missed her. Never before had he felt such emptiness. It was a longing he did not understand.

He made a small camp in the open space between two groups of dwellings. He used his cloak over poles for a lean-to and gathered stones for a fireplace. Small animals and birds would be his food while he kept his vigil. Keeping solitary watches was easy for him.

On the evening of the fourth night, he looked up from his cooking fire and saw a familiar group approaching.

He quickly stomped out the fire and dismantled his shelter.

"Hello, Hedad," he shouted.

"Hello, Firingin." Hedad seemed to be in better spirits. "We did well with the sale of the yearlings," he said, "and water is cheap in Korr. Twelve of the camels have been loaded with water and salt, and I have money left. By letting the two hired drivers go their way, I will save even more."

"Did you see any police?" Firingin said.

"Yes. And they asked if I had seen the white woman."

"And what did you tell them?"

Hedad smiled. "I told the truth," he said. "What would you expect?"

Firingin waited. Hedad must be making a joke.

"I told them I had not seen any white people since I left my village." Hedad laughed. He laughed, and Firingin laughed with him.

Firingin laughed, but he knew what Hedad's report meant. The police had expanded their search to the desert. His hand drifted to the handle of his knife. He touched it, and he knew what he had to do. As soon as the caravan reached the village, he and Leslie would start the long trip back.

Nearly a month had passed since Firingin had left, and Leslie still had difficulty adjusting. Her vomiting had stopped, but she'd become more concerned about medical care. She had never seen anything close to a doctor—not even a witch doctor—around the village. How did these women have their babies?

When she asked Wambila, her friend told her they had mid-wives. "All of our children are delivered by women in the village," Wambila said. "I, myself, am a midwife. I haven't lost a normal baby yet."

Leslie tried eating richer food. She choked down bowls of the yogurt and even drank some of the blood-milk mixture she'd asked Wambila to bring.

Leslie had gagged on the first swallow but kept drinking. She'd reasoned that he needed nourishment more than she needed a tranquil stomach.

She thought of the baby as he now—a sort of substitute for his missing father.

As the days mounted beyond a month, it became increasingly difficult for Leslie to concentrate on her school. Each shout from the corral, each whistle from a herdsman made her drop her lesson in mid-sentence and go to the doorway. From a distance, she glared at the faces of the drivers of each arriving herd until she was certain that Firingin was not among them.

When she returned to the class circle, no doubt showing disappointment, some of her students would start whispering. She worried that they would report her strange behavior to their mothers. Even Wambila seemed to be avoiding her. It must be close to the time for Jeiso to be told.

Leslie only hoped that her friend would give her warning—not that she knew what she would do with the advanced notice.

One morning Wambila interrupted the school and asked Leslie to come outside. The tall woman's expression was grave, and her eyes examined Leslie's face as though she had not seen it, before.

This is it, Leslie thought, but she said nothing.

"There is word from the corral," Wambila said. "Keigo, a driver from Hedad's caravan, just rode in. He told some of the herders about an accident."

Leslie opened her mouth, but speech didn't come.

Wambila continued. "Keigo wouldn't say what kind of accident. But we won't have long to wait."

"Why is that?"

"The caravan is coming home. He said it should be here in a few days."

Leslie trembled. She didn't know if she should be happy or if everything in her new life had now collapsed.

If Firingin had been killed, what would happen to her and

her baby? She stared at Wambila. "The driver didn't say anything about Firingin?"

"No. The boy from the corral said he wouldn't give any details. After he unloaded his camel, he went directly to Jeiso's lodge."

Leslie looked across the courtyard at the old man's dwelling. She returned her gaze to Wambila.

"And have you gone to Jeiso?" she whispered.

"About your problem?"

Leslie nodded.

"Not yet," Wambila said. "I can wait a few more days."

29

On the transit to Ilaut, the caravan moved slowly. The camels complained under their loads, and Hedad allowed frequents stops. He seemed to be transformed back to his happy self and even ordered a overnight stop at the end of their first day.

Firingin said little around the campfire. The boys talked of the usual nonsense around the meal, and Hedad laughed with them. The camels had been unloaded, a laborious process with the water carriers, and they were hobbled nearby. Keigo set up the sentry schedule, using the boys for all but the first shift. Firingin volunteered for that.

Walking in the moonlight among the grazing beasts, he thought of his future. He would return Leslie, but what then? He would not be welcomed back to Jeiso's village after the old one found out about his treachery.

And he'd already decided that the Lbaa would not accept him. Maybe he should surrender to the police. What he had done was in his own defense. He might be able to explain that.

A camel bolted out of its tether, and Firingin ran to stop its flight. He thought no more about the puzzles of his future.

The town of Ilaut seemed as tranquil as it had been the time before, so Firingin entered with the caravan. His help unloading the salt and water and loading replacement bags of fodder would be appreciated.

While in the settlement, he went to the store and purchased all the paper and pencils on the shelf. Leslie would have little need for them now, but he wanted to see her smile.

After four days in Ilaut, the caravan left for South Horr. Everybody talked of returning home. The boy drivers laughed and sang from their positions at the rear of the column. It had been a long time for them to be on the road, but they had survived and seemed to be feeling pleased with themselves.

Hedad at the head of the train remained in good spirits. He had sold water for a profit and would make more when he sold grain and salt to the Turkana. The expedition had been away days longer than planned, but Jeiso would be grateful for the shillings they would bring.

A day later, when the caravan was crossing a large, open basin, Firingin noticed one of the camels lift its nose skyward and sniff.

"What's ahead?" he yelled.

"They must smell ghosts in the wind," Hedad yelled back.

Strange beasts. They were tough enough to march a week without water but were sensitive to unseen vapors in the air.

A short time later, a camel at the rear of the line bolted and ripped loose from its rope. The load shifted as the beast jumped sideways. One of the young drivers yelled for a halt.

Hedad stopped the lead camel. "Hurry," he said. He pointed to a ridgeline ahead. "That cliff could hide bandits."

The caravan had entered Turkana territory, and Hedad had grown nervous.

Firingin assisted the young herder by holding the jumpy animal. The load was secured and the beast hitched back into line. The caravan promptly started.

The wind picked up, and the animals kept bucking as they walked. Hedad called for another stop after several loads came lose.

Firingin looked at the sky. It remained cloudless, but the light had dimmed. Particles of dust floated high above.

"A sandstorm is coming," Hedad yelled. "Be alert for a blackout."

Firingin had never seen a blackout. In Samburu country, the roots of trees and the grass kept most of the soil in its place—even against the strongest winds.

"If it comes our way," Hedad shouted over the sound of the blowing, "we will circle the beasts."

"We should hobble them now," Keigo yelled, but Hedad didn't answer.

Another camel bolted, and one of the boys grabbed its rope before it broke loose. Firingin moved closer to the line. Sand pelted his face and arms, and he could barely see Hedad through the dust.

Keigo had moved in close on the opposite side. Only two of the boys were visible behind. Firingin couldn't see the third anywhere.

"Do you see Jeido?" Firingin yelled to Keigo. Keigo did not answer. The storm blew too hard.

Firingin grabbed the lead-rope of the camel beside him. He worked his way forward from beast to beast. He needed to tell Hedad about losing sight of the boy.

Each camel jumped and kicked when Firingin grabbed its load carrier. More cargo bags had shifted on their frames, but he wouldn't stop to fix them.

"We must stop," he yelled, when he reached the front of the column.

"Ahead is a sheltering cliff," Hedad bellowed. "We will form a circle beside it."

"I think Jeido is lost."

"Lost?"

"He is not visible behind."

"We can't stop yet."

Firingin couldn't see the cliff ahead. Thick dust had filled the air. He couldn't see anything but the back of Hedad's cloak and the nearby head of the lead camel. He linked his arm through the rope of the old she-camel's halter and grabbed her rein. Hedad's hand was also on the rein.

Now Firingin saw only darkness. He wrapped his cape across his face and held it with his free hand.

"We must stop!" he yelled toward Hedad's hand.

It kept pulling.

Firingin saw a ball of thorns come out of the blackness and hit the side of the lead camel. The animal bolted, throwing her head from side to side. Her halter-rope dug into Firingin's arm, but it held him to her head.

The rein in front had whipped free. Hedad's hand was not on it.

Firingin shouted for his cousin and tried to jam his heels into the ground. If he did not stop the lead camel's rampage, she would take the caravan with its animals and cargo on a mindless charge into the storm.

Hedad would be lost in the desert behind.

Firingin wrapped his cape over the camel's face and clucked to her ear. After a time, she stopped her jumping. He pulled her head against his side and covered her eyes to calm her. She stood still for a moment and then kneeled down.

With his arm still in her halter, Firingin was pulled down beside her head. The storm raged and he kept clucking. He felt tugs on the lead camel's harness.

Other camels must still be pulling against the wind.

Eventually, the tugging stopped. They had broken free or were also settling down.

An hour or more of sand and dirt piled against Firingin and the she-camel. Then the storm ended.

Slowly the air cleared. The sound of bawling animals replaced the howling wind.

Firingin patted the lead camel's neck and released her halter. She pushed herself to her feet. Firingin stood and threw off his robe. A shower of sand scattered to the ground. He surveyed the scene.

Animals and men emerged from nearby and distant mounds of debris. Behind the lead camel, four of her followers rose from the sand. Two even had bags of grain attached to their cargo carriers. Some of the bags were leaking, and Firingin quickly tied them shut.

He saw Keigo come from behind a shelter of boulders with two animals in tow.

"Have you seen Hedad?" Firingin asked. Keigo shook his head. "Two of the boys are behind me with six more beasts."

"Watch these," Firingin said. "I will look for Hedad."

At first, it was only a scrap of cloth that he saw, fluttering from the large mound. The pattern of Hedad's cape waving in the stillness had caught his eye and stopped his walking.

He ran to the cloth and dug around it with his hands. The swatch of color lead downward into the sand.

"Hedad!" he yelled. "Help me. Help me dig."

His fingers touched the body. It didn't move!

Like a crazy man, he scratched at the debris until he uncovered a shoulder, then the neck and finally the head.

Hedad's eyes stared from the pit. They were open, filled with grains of sand. But they did not see.

Firingin felt tears start to flow. He looked at the sky to stop them and saw Keigo.

"Is he dead?" Keigo's asked.

Firingin nodded. He pointed to the bruise on Hedad's temple. He cleared his throat. "Must have hit the rock."

With Keigo's help, he worked Hedad's body free from its

sandy grave. "Bring one of the beasts," he said to Keigo. "We will take him to his wife."

"One of the boys is also missing," Keigo said. "The others say they heard him calling early in the storm."

"We will camp and look for him," Firingin said. "Tomorrow you must take a camel and ride to Jeiso's village. Tell the old one, nobody else, what has happened. Let Jeiso tell Hedad's woman."

Stories about the accident circulated everywhere in the village. Keigo had said nothing, but speculation ran rampant. Some of the tales were wild: sinkholes that swallowed the camels and drivers whole or Turkana that had swept down on the caravan, butchering man and beast alike.

Wambila laughed. "People dream up these demons," she said. "They forget that the caravan is on its way home. It has not been destroyed."

"But why doesn't Jeiso just tell the people what happened?" Leslie said.

"It is not his way," Wambila replied.

The second day after Keigo's return, Leslie closed her school. She couldn't think about lessons at a time like this.

She went to the corral, hoping to hear some news.

She tried to listen to the conversations but had trouble understanding the herders' fast talking. Also, it seemed the boys were afraid of her. If they knew anything, she'd be the last one they'd tell. After nearly an hour in the glaring sunshine, she gave up and returned to her dwelling. From her doorway, she would keep a watch on the trail to the west.

She kept her vigil, except for brief moments, through the next full day.

In mid-afternoon, she saw it. At first a speck on the horizon but then clearly a caravan, a line of camels in the wavy distance and drivers along side.

She waited until it came close. Once, the first day, she'd charged from her circle of students and across the courtyard, only to discover the camels were a herd returning from the waterhole.

As today's procession approached the far circle of dwellings, she recognized the gait of the driver in front. His strides were long and his posture tall and regal. The driver was definitely Firingin!

She started running. Again, abandoning caution, she raced from her hut and toward the stretch of open desert.

When she passed Wambila's dwelling, her friend ran out.

"Leslie! Where are you going?" Wambila shouted.

Leslie halted but kept dancing with excitement.

"They're coming, Wambila," she said. "I see Hedad's caravan coming from the west."

She turned back to the line of camels.

"Don't go out there, Leslie," Wambila said.

"Why not? It's them."

Wambila came and stood beside her. "Their camels have been a long time on the trail. You could cause a stampede."

Leslie looked at the caravan and nodded. She didn't want to do something that was stupid.

"Let's go to the corral," Wambila added. "That's where they're headed."

"Firingin is alive," Leslie said. "I can tell that it's him walking in front."

Wambila studied the caravan. "Yes, Firingin is the leader. I wonder what's happened to Hedad?"

The column of twelve animals moved past them on its way to the village corral. Leslie restrained herself as she watched Firingin.

His eyes were fixed straight ahead.

The dusty train of animals loped by. Over the back of the last camel, Leslie saw the body of a man.

With arms hanging stiffly, he was obviously dead!

Leslie could hardly contain her emotions when a half-hour later, Firingin walked solemnly through the opening in the barricade. In front of all the assembled people, she ran to him, shamelessly.

"Hello," she said. Tears streamed down her cheeks.

She hated it when she cried.

He looked beyond her toward the village. He seemed barely to notice her!

When he looked down, all he said was, "Hedad is dead."

At least he spoke. A commotion by the corral drew her attention. At the gap in the stick fence, two youths struggled with a large blanket-covered bundle.

"The boys bring his body," Firingin said.

She wrapped her arm around his back. "It must have been awful," she said. "What happened?"

"A storm. Hedad fell and was killed. Jeido, Jeiso's great-grandson, is lost. We searched but could not find him."

"Keigo rode into the village three days ago," she said, "but he didn't talk much."

"Yes," Firingin said. "I sent him to tell Jeiso."

He looked again toward the village and then at the crowd of people. Some of the bystanders asked questions, but Firingin didn't answer.

Leslie tried to hug him with both arms. "I'm so glad you're back," she said.

He pulled away. "I must speak to Jeiso," he said, "but I do not see him."

Leslie looked around. "He's probably in his lodge. He hasn't been in the courtyard since Keigo came back."

"Keigo? He is not here either."

"He's been in his hut since he talked to Jeiso. Some say he sleeps."

Firingin walked toward the central area of the village. Leslie walked beside him. "Come," she said, "let's go home."

"I must speak to Jeiso," Firingin said. "Then I will come. We have things to talk about."

She nodded. "We certainly do."

Firingin stopped in front of the patriarch's lodge.

The boys who had followed behind laid their bundle at the doorway. Firingin went inside, and the boys went with him.

Leslie watched for a moment and then went to her own dwelling.

Even from her doorway, Leslie could smell the rotting body. The desert heat had obviously accelerated the process.

It grew dark. The milkers and herders came from the corral, and still Firingin remained in Jeiso's lodge.

Only once had he emerged. With Jeiso, he had come out and had removed something from the corpse.

Leslie stayed by her doorway, using her wrap to shield the putrid odor from her nose. Finally she closed her eyes. The exhaustion of the three-day vigil had caught up to her. She slept.

A shake of her shoulder woke her.

She rubbed her eyes. "Hello," she said. It was Firingin. "Are you finished?"

He nodded. Before he sat down, he handed her a package. "I brought the paper and pencils," he said.

She turned the bundle over in her hands. "You remembered. Through all that trauma, you still remembered."

"You are lucky," he said. "The camel that carried this package did not lose its load."

She crawled to light the lantern and then opened the

wrapper. "And you got the colored ones!"

He grinned.

She laid her head against his shoulder. "I do love you," she said. Her eyes were wet again.

He stroked her leg, and her pulse quickened.

His hands moved to her breasts. She felt herself falling into delicious abandon. "Come," she said and pulled him toward her.

After the most wonderful intercourse, she snuggled beside him.

He had rolled on his back and laid looking at the ceiling. There would never be a better time to tell him.

"I have some wonderful news for you," she said.

He turned on his side and stared at her. He looked like he hadn't even heard. "You must return," he said.

"What! I don't understand you," she replied. "Why are you saying that now?"

"The police..."

"So what about the police?" she asked. "They don't matter any more. We've got something more important to talk about."

He looked frustrated. "The police are in Korr," he said. "Hedad talked to them."

"So what? I've got something to tell you, Firingin," she practically shouted. "We're going to have a baby."

The urgency of her tone must have finally gotten his attention. He sat up and looked at her.

"A baby?" he said.

"Yes. And even if there are police, I can't go back now," she said. "I couldn't make such a trip with a baby."

He stood up, bumping his head against the roof and knelt back on the blankets, rubbing his hair.

"It cannot be," he finally said. "We are not married."

"That's what Wambila said when I told her. But I promised her we would get married when you got back."

He looked angry.

"You will, won't you?" she said. She hated the pleading sound of her question. She tried to explain. "Wambila says they'll kill our child if we don't."

He looked at the floor and said nothing.

"Firingin!" she said. "They'll kill our child. Don't you care?"

He said nothing, and she felt real panic. What would she do? He didn't even care.

She picked up the pencils and threw them across the room. "Shit!" she screamed. Once again she was crying.

He looked at her with sad eyes. "I cannot marry," he said. "In my tribe, I am not a man."

She dried her eyes. "That's crazy," she said. "When your aunt told me that, I couldn't believe it. I couldn't believe then, and I definitely don't believe it now. If you're not a man, I don't know who would be."

He reached over and felt her stomach. She pulled back. "No!" she said, "not now."

He touched her again. "How do you know there is a baby?" he said. "I feel nothing."

What a strange man. Now he was interested. She felt herself smile. "It is early," she said. "But I have felt the life inside me."

He crawled to the opening of the dwelling and looked out at the darkness. "I do not know the ways of the Rendille," he said. "When the time is right, I will talk to Jeiso about marriage among his people."

"No!" she said, "You can't talk to Jeiso. He can't find out about this baby."

"I must talk to him. If we are to be married, it must be done according to tribal rules. There is no other way."

She clasped her hands and thought. "OK," she said, "talk about the wedding. But don't tell him I'm pregnant."

"After Hedad's funeral, I will talk to Jeiso. Many things must be discussed."

"What things?"

"I will speak to him about the police. He must be told."

"No! Don't tell him that. He'll make us leave."

"But he should know of the danger."

"There is no danger. Believe me, the police will soon give up their searching. There might have been some media attention at first, but people have short attention spans. It's been over two months. No police will keep looking in this desert more than two months."

She might have gotten a little carried away with her supposed knowledge of law enforcement practices, but Firingin seemed ready to believe. "How do you know these things?" he said.

"Everyone in America knows such things."

Firingin smiled. "It is true. Korr is far. Perhaps the police will stay there."

"So what other things do you have to discuss?"

"If we will be married, I must find out how many animals I must pay. I must be told who to pay. I do not even know the man who is your father."

"My father's dead."

"So it might be your uncle, I pay."

"Firingin, it doesn't matter," she said. His insistence on all these tribal things was almost humorous. "My father or my uncle. Nobody cares. My people don't believe in selling women."

"The Rendille will say," he said. "We must follow their rules."

"All right. But promise you won't tell Jeiso about the baby."

"Does no one in the village know?"

"Only Wambila. She has given her word to keep silent."

"Then I will not tell him."

31

Four boys from the village carried Hedad's body to the desert. There had been no ceremony. Without children, Hedad did not rate formal recognition. Jeiso had given a short talk, invoking a blessing from Wak, and he had waved the remains out of the courtyard.

Within a few days, scavengers—vultures, hyenas and jackals—will have consumed all but the memory of Firingin's cousin.

Jeiso asked Firingin to talk to Hedad's wife. Firingin felt obligated, and even though he'd never talked to the woman, he'd agreed.

When he approached her dwelling, he noticed that it was completely silent. He looked through the doorway and in the dimness saw her, sitting on the blankets.

"I am Firingin," he said.

"I know you," she replied. "Come in."

"I have come to speak of Hedad."

"Hedad?"

"Yes, your dead husband. Jeiso asked me to tell you about the day of his death."

"He's dead?"

Did the woman not know? It was true she had not been among those who listened to Jeiso's words. Firingin considered returning to the old one with this new information.

"Come tell me," she said.

He sat before her. "It was during a sand storm," he said. "He was…"

The woman had placed her hand on his body. "Go on," she said.

Firingin felt uncomfortable. This woman had been married to his friend. He resumed. "Hedad was leading the caravan." He stopped again. The woman had removed her wrap and had stretched her body before him.

He backed toward the doorway.

"Don't go," she said. He saw the glisten of tears in her eyes. She was smooth of skin, but he would not accept her invitation.

"Please, you must not do this," he said. "Hedad was my friend. I saw his hand reaching from the sand."

She turned herself toward him. "Come," she said.

He felt the arousal, but he shook his head. "I will not."

"Come, give me a child," she said. "They will think it is his."

He saw her need. Without children, she had no honor as a Rendille widow. "I cannot," he said. "I have my own woman."

"I will live in poverty," she said. "Come, give me a son."

"Jeiso will help you," he said. "He loved Hedad."

Before she could make another request, he left her dwelling.

Without looking back, Firingin returned to Leslie's dwelling. There he slept, and after he was rested, he sat in the back of room. He watched Leslie as she searched for the pencils she had thrown in her anger. When she found all of them, she said, she would again start her school.

He watched Leslie and tried to imagine the baby she carried. Would it be a thin-skin like her or would it be like him? Maybe it would be an ugly combination of both—perhaps spotted with light and dark skin. He had never seen a baby that wasn't totally of his race.

When he voiced his concern, Leslie laughed.

"Spotted!" She said. "That's crazy. Don't you know anything about babies?"

He rubbed his head. Of course he knew.

Leslie continued. "I've seen dozens of children with one black parent and one white. Sometimes they've been light colored and sometimes dark but never spotted. Where do you get such ideas?"

He shrugged. Her answer had made him feel better about the baby but worse about himself. He crawled to the opening of the dwelling. He would go to the corral.

Before he could leave, Leslie asked her daily question. "Have you spoken to Jeiso?"

He shook his head. "It is too soon. He still grieves for Hedad."

She patted her stomach. "Don't keep putting it off."

The following morning, Leslie restarted the school.

As soon as the morning meal was finished, students came into the dwelling. Firingin went to the courtyard and watched the old ones.

Jeiso seemed unhappy. While Firingin watched, the old patriarch's opponent beat him once. When another man started to take the lead in the next contest, Jeiso suddenly dumped the board. "I cannot play with fools," he said.

He stood and looked at Firingin. "Come, Grandson. Come smoke with me."

When they entered Jeiso's dwelling, the old one shooed out a lingering wife.

"She always lurks near the fireplace," he said. "She wants to hear my secrets."

He motioned Firingin to the carpeted smoking area and slowly packed the water-pipe.

Firingin stretched out and watched as Jeiso drew hard on the stem. The old one exhaled a large cloud of smoke and closed his eyes. Firingin waited.

Jeiso took another drag and handed the stem to Firingin. Firingin took a puff and handed it back. The smoke of Jeiso's Turkish tobacco was mild to the throat.

Jeiso leaned across the fireplace and touched the handle of Firingin's knife. The old one smiled.

"Once, years ago," he said, "a headsman from a distant village came to me and wanted to trade camels."

Firingin made no reply. Jeiso leaned back and gazed at the opening in the roof. "The headsman had a beautiful knife." Jeiso winked. "It was not as beautiful as yours, but it put my own poor blade to shame."

Jeiso struggled with his robes and withdrew his weapon. He placed it, handle toward Firingin, on the stones of the fireplace. The knife was indeed plain with handle of common wood, a steel band at the base and a steel cap at the top.

"I could not trade camels with that man," Jeiso said. "His knife was so beautiful, I was ashamed to bargain with him. It was years before I found another trader with camels so valuable."

Jeiso took in another drag of smoke and reached again for Firingin's knife. He nodded and smiled as his fingers stroked the rhino horn. "It is said that horn of a rhinoceros brings sex to an old man," Jeiso said.

Firingin drew the jeweled weapon from its holder. He saw Jeiso's eyes gleam with desire.

Firingin felt the cavity in the gold band. He looked at the watery eyes that stared at the object in his hand. He owed Jeiso much, but would he bring harm rather than pleasure if he gave him the knife he coveted? Would the blemish in the handle somehow put his generous grandfather at risk.

He gazed at the smoke drifting above their heads.

Leslie had been sure that the police would not come, and she seemed to know their ways. Perhaps he worried too much about risks.

He laid his knife on the hearthstones with its handle toward Jeiso. "It is not good for the leader of a great family to feel ashamed of his weapon," Firingin said.

Jeiso grabbed the jeweled handle. He turned it several times in his hands and carefully placed the blade in his own scabbard.

Firingin picked up the knife that remained on the fireplace.

Jeiso took another draw on his pipe. "Hedad was a good driver," he said. Jeiso now seemed ready for casual conversation.

Firingin nodded.

"He was one of my best," Jeiso added.

"He knew how to handle his beasts and also the Ethiopian traders," Firingin replied.

Jeiso nodded. "It will be difficult to replace one so skillful."

They smoked, trading the stem back and forth.

"You will be the one," Jeiso finally said. "You are my eldest grandson. It is right that you lead Hedad's caravan."

Firingin coughed out a cloud of smoke and coughed again before he spoke, "But I am Samburu, Grandfather. I do not know the ways of a Rendille trader."

Jeiso laughed. He laughed until he wheezed. Firingin had forgotten how the old man laughed at him.

Jeiso wiped his mouth and stopped. "The Samburu who thinks he is your father is a fool," he said.

"I do not understand," Firingin said. "Why do you say thinks he is my father? My mother, your daughter, is married to him in the clan of the Lbaa. It is true the father is a foolish man, but I am his eldest son."

"But he is not your father," Jeiso said. "The daughter I sold to him carried another man's child. You, her eldest, are the one she carried."

Firingin stared at Jeiso's face. The old one had said words that rang strange in his ears. It was difficult to comprehend the meaning. If he was not a child of the father, who was his male-parent?

"The man, my father," Firingin said. "Does he live in this village?"

Jeiso looked at him carefully. The patriarch seemed to be searching his memory for the answer. He took another drag, and when he exhaled, he smiled.

"No," he said. "But that man is known to me. He lives in a village to the north."

"He is Rendille then?"

"Yes. And you, my grandson, are also Rendille."

Firingin felt a weight lift from his chest. With that one, simple sentence, his life had been completely changed. The rules of the father's tribe were no longer Firingin's rules. The Samburu decision to make him forever a child was not real.

He looked through the dwelling's doorway at the brightness of the courtyard. He felt himself smile, and he let his smile widened to a grin. He was a Rendille!

Not a Samburu and not a child-herder of beasts.

"Grandfather," he said. "I wish to marry the woman, the one known as Leslie."

Jeiso nodded. "It is right that you should. I have seen the way she looks at you, and I have also seen the hunger of Hedad's widow. It is time for you to have your own family."

Firingin wondered if Jeiso already had plans for his second wedding. He would not marry Hedad's former wife, but he would talk of it later.

"The woman Leslie wishes to marry me and to live in this village," he said. "She also wants to continue teaching the children in her school."

"That is right, too," Jeiso said. "The world changes. Our children must know the ways of the world."

"If I am Rendille, as you say, we might marry in this village, but I know nothing of the traditions. Among the Samburu, I was not in the age set of men who could marry."

"Such foolishness. You are not Samburu. You do not live by their age sets. I know your years. When you brought Hedad's caravan to me, you proved yourself a man in my village."

"But I have no beasts. How can I pay for the woman?"

Jeiso lit his pipe and inhaled deeply. He exhaled and looked at Firingin. "It is true. Rendille law requires the payment of eight camels for a wife."

"I have none."

"You returned twelve of Hedad's camels to me."

"True, but they are yours."

"Eight of those will be for your woman."

"How can I pay for her with your camels?" Firingin said.

"The camels are mine, my grandson," Jeiso said. "But you brought them from the desert to me. When you did you gave me the eight and four more. They were your payment. And after you are married, they will be waiting for you to drive in my caravan."

Firingin frowned. Jeiso was a generous man, but he never missed getting what he wanted.

"Do not let your face be sad," Jeiso said. "Keigo will help you with the caravan until he grows too old. When he sits in the courtyard, you will be skilled as the leader. Now, bring a smile to your eyes and bring your woman to me. My number one wife will attend to her."

"Attend to me! What does that mean?" Leslie said when Firingin gave her Jeiso's instructions.

He shrugged and stirred his yogurt. Already, Leslie spoke as a wife. "I do not know the ceremonial rules," he said. "Perhaps she will prepare you for the circumcision."

"Circumcision!" Leslie screamed. "Are you crazy? That's for men."

He nodded. His patience was being tried by this conversation. "For women too," he said. "Samburu women must be circumcised for marriage. It may be the same for Rendille women."

Leslie shuddered. "I can't even imagine such a thing. What do they remove?"

"I have not watched it," he said. "A piece from inside, I think."

"The clitoris," she said. "Oh, my God!"

He did not know the word, so he said nothing and waited for her anger to subside.

"Tell old Jeiso," she said in a husky voice, "that it's not happening this time. Not with this woman."

"I will not tell him," Firingin said. It was time for him to assume the man's authority. "If you will not present yourself, you must be the one to tell him."

"I will then," she said. She dumped the yogurt from her bowl into the fire. "I hate that stuff."

He waited again until the anger had left her eyes.

"Jeiso told me that I am not Samburu," he said. "He said my mother carried me before she was married."

Leslie looked at him, and a smile spread slowly over her face. "Now that's rich," Leslie said. She often used such phrases when she was excited. "And all this stuff about you not being a man—it's gone, too?"

He nodded. "Jeiso wants me to lead Hedad's caravan."

"But you can't, can you? You can't go to places like this Korr. The police may still be there."

"But you said we didn't have to worry about the police."

"Well, that's true," she said. "But still you ought to be careful."

"Jeiso says that Keigo will help me. He can take the camels into Korr."

"Do you have to?" she said.

"I cannot refuse. Jeiso would not understand."

Her face looked sad. He did not understand, but they went

to the blankets. Soon her eyes glistened.

In the days that followed, Firingin stayed around the corral. He groomed the camels that would be his to drive and talked to Keigo about future expeditions. The language of boys working near the pens was still hard to understand, but they now respected him and listened carefully to his instructions. He walked proudly among those tending the beasts—he'd become a man among other men.

Leslie talked to Jeiso, and the old one had assured her that she would not be circumcised. Her face was now happy, and Firingin once more enjoyed his evening meals.

Each day he woke up to a feeling of joy. He was already a respected member of the community, and after five more days had passed, the woman named Leslie would be his number one wife.

32

Leslie swatted at the fly that kept buzzing around her face. She missed it, and the children laughed. They didn't seem to understand why it bothered her.

She settled into her spot at the head of the circle.

Expectant eyes of her students tracked her hands as she sorted through the sheets for the day's lesson. She loved these children. They wanted so much to learn what she had to teach.

Leslie loved teaching, but it was only one of the many things she liked about her new life. As the wife of Jeiso's eldest grandson, soon to bear the old one another heir, she had acquired a place of respect in the village.

Never before had Leslie lived where she had so many friends and admirers. She couldn't walk across the courtyard without someone stopping her to talk. She understood most of what they said. After three months in the community, even parts of the Rendille dialect had meaning.

Except for certain items of food, crawly things in the desert, and the incessant flies, she couldn't have asked for a more satisfying existence. The desert air had even cleared up most of her sinus problems, and the constant looking at distant views had given strength to eyes.

She passed out the daily arithmetic assignment and watched while the students started work. When they all seemed to be settled in, Leslie crawled to the doorway.

She needed to go outside and stretch her legs. Sitting on the floor was the worst thing about teaching, especially now that she was beginning to feel the discomfort of her pregnancy.

She stood up and smoothed her wrap over the slight bulge in her abdomen. She had no fear of exposing her condition—even in the open courtyard. The wedding had removed all threat of a forced abortion.

A few days after the ceremonies, Wambila had come by the dwelling and offered her services as a mid-wife. She would do more for Leslie than simply attend the delivery. Wambila's knowledge of pre-natal care in the environs of the desert community was both helpful and comforting.

Leslie heard shouts from the corral. Perhaps it was Firingin and his young herders taking the camels to the northern watering hole. He'd told her that morning that he'd be going there. She made Firingin tell her each day what he would do. She had so much still to learn about their life.

Every day he went to the corral. With Keigo and the boys who helped, Firingin tended the camels of Hedad's caravan. Like a gentle parent, he fed, watered, and groomed each individual animal. Clearly, Firingin enjoyed working with the beasts—it was the name he and every one else used for the livestock.

While the camels of caravan took up most of his time, the pregnant young she-camel that Jeiso had given him as a wedding present was his special interest. The young female would give birth about the same time Leslie expected to have the baby. She wondered, sometimes, which pregnancy interested her husband the most.

She shook her head. She didn't want to be gloomy. There would be plenty of time to feel sorry for herself next week. It was then that Firingin would leave on his first caravan expedition. It would be a water-and-salt run to South Horr and Ilaut. He'd told her that they wouldn't be away as long as before, but still she worried. Stories about caravan accidents were rampant among the women of the village. At least she wouldn't have to worry about creepy things at night. Jeiso had already introduced the warriors who would guard her dwelling. They wore red capes but otherwise scarcely resembled the fierce spear-carriers of the Samburu.

Leslie saw Wambila coming across the courtyard. It was her best friend's day to help with the lunches. She carried several leather bags of food under her arms.

"What are you doing outside?" Wambila said.

"I needed to stand up for a few minutes."

"Well, don't leave me in there alone," Wambila said. "I might have to kill a couple of those wild boys."

Leslie smiled. "I don't understand. They're just fine with me."

"You're still a celebrity. Wait another month or two."

Wambila crawled into the dwelling, and Leslie followed.

"I think I'll take the class outside," Leslie said. "These flies are too thick."

"They're everywhere," Wambila said. "I think it must be a new hatching."

"Yuk," Leslie said and waved the students through the doorway. The wind blew across the courtyard as it always did. It would keep away the insects. She usually had classes in the open when paperwork wasn't involved.

The children took their places, and Leslie sat down on the cargo carrier Firingin had brought from the corral. "How about a story before lunch?" she said.

The small ones jumped up and down and yelled their approval.

"What would you like to hear?" she asked. She knew what the answer would be. Again they would want to hear about life in America.

Leslie had just gotten into her tale about the dairy farm in Ohio when she heard the sound. It was soft at first, but it grew quickly. The whopping was coming directly toward the village!

The children stood and looked in the direction of the noise. They looked at each other and then at Leslie.

"Go inside!" she said.

She'd heard the sound of helicopters many times in the past. If, as she feared, these machines carried the police, it could soon become violent in the courtyard.

Leslie remained in front of the dwelling and watched the two dark aircraft coming from the southeast.

They flew close to the ground, raising dust as they approached.

Camels bellowed in the corral. Leslie could hear the herders shouting to keep their charges from stampeding the barricades.

One helicopter climbed as it came close. It circled high overhead, and the other banked for a landing in the courtyard. Clouds of sand swept across the area as the machine chattered downward. Skins blew from the roofs of several nearby dwellings.

The people of the village ran for cover. Some screamed as they crowded into their doorways. Others looked with curiosity from where they crouched behind the shelter of the huts.

Leslie looked toward Jeiso's dwelling. The old patriarch was standing in front, holding his hands, palms out, over his head. She knew he was terrified and went to his side.

The helicopter pivoted to its touch down, and Leslie shouted to be heard over its roar.

"They come for me," she said.

Jeiso didn't seem to hear. "What are these devils?" he shouted. From her experience with the Rendille people, she knew that the devils he asked about were spiritual, not condemnatory. She grabbed his arm. It trembled in her grip.

"These are men, not devils," she said. "I will talk to them."

Two soldiers dismounted from the bubble cockpit, followed by one civilian. The civilian was Sammy!

Leslie patted Jeiso's wrist. "I know one of them," she said. She advanced a few steps and stopped to watch as the soldiers directed Sammy under the swinging blades.

Sammy looked worried.

"Stay here," Leslie said to Jeiso, and she walked toward the tour driver.

"Sammy," she said and waved.

He waved back and held out his hand to her. She reached and the two gripped hands like old friends. The green-clad soldiers stood and watched. One held an automatic rifle at the ready.

"How did you find this place?" she asked.

Sammy nodded his head toward one of the soldiers.

"The chief inspector knew where it was."

The second, larger helicopter landed outside the ring of huts. Its descent scattered the people from that side of the village.

A half-dozen armed troopers climbed out of the giant machine and advanced toward the courtyard. One by one, they searched the dwellings. People ran from their homes and were stopped by the weapon-toting officers.

"What are they doing?" Leslie said. "These villagers aren't hiding anything."

"They search for a murderer," the officer beside Sammy said. "We think he is here."

So they were coming as Firingin had feared. Her mind raced, trying to think of what to say. "That's nonsense," she blurted out. "I've been here over three months. There's been no murder."

"The murder was not committed here," the officer said. "In Maralal one of our men was killed. We believe the killer is the one who brought you here."

Leslie was taken aback. How could they know so much? Again, she tried to think of a good response.

"The man who brought me here is my husband," she almost shouted. "Not a killer of policemen."

Inside she quivered with almost uncontrollable fright. What if Firingin returned at this moment?

Sammy talked to the tall officer. They both looked at her, and Sammy shook his head. She couldn't tell if his expression showed disbelief or disgust.

"You must get your things," he said. "The chief inspector says his men will soon complete their search. He wants to leave when they are finished."

She looked away at the horizon. "That's fine, go," she said without looking back. "But I'm not going with you."

Sammy looked flustered. "You must," he said. "The chief inspector has orders from the highest authorities in Nairobi."

"I don't care about his orders," she said. "I'm not leaving."

Sammy turned to the tall officer. They spoke in rapid Swahili. When Sammy looked again at Leslie, he said, "Chief-Inspector Wanjau says you must come. He says you will not be charged with any crime if you come peacefully."

She shook her head. The officer with the gun stepped forward and poked the muzzle in her back.

Jeiso shuffled toward the group. He must have felt it was time to come to her defense. He hurled curses at the officers in his own language and seemed to be reaching for his knife.

She held up her hands. "No, Jeiso," she said. "I'm not in danger."

She turned and glared at the officer holding the gun. She spoke in the strongest tone she could muster.

"Take your gun away," she said. She looked at Sammy.

"Tell the chief inspector that I'm an American citizen, and I don't care what his orders are. If he takes me back as a prisoner, he'd better be prepared for the howl I'll raise with the United States Embassy."

Sammy spoke again to the senior officer. The chief-inspector looked puzzled. They said more, and the officer nodded. He spoke to Leslie in slow English. "I'll not force you to go, but I will need a signed statement from you."

"Bring me paper, and I'll give you one," Leslie said.

The officer waved the gun-toting soldier toward the helicopter. The pilot reached behind his seat and handed out a clipboard and a pen.

When the chief-inspector handed Leslie the paper, he pointed to the bottom of the sheet. "Date it, please, by your signature," he said.

She hurriedly wrote: I FREELY ELECT TO STAY IN THIS VILLAGE. I HAVE BEEN OFFERED SAFE RETURN BY THESE OFFICERS AND HAVE REFUSED IT. I AM HAPPY WHERE I AM.

She scrawled her signature and looked at Sammy.

"What is the date?" she asked.

"September 22," he said "19..."

"I assume the year hasn't changed," she said. "Why does he want it, anyhow?"

Sammy shook his head, again. "What you do is not wise," he said.

"What I do is my business," she replied. She handed the clipboard to the chief inspector.

"You make a big mistake, Leslie," Sammy said. "These police will be back. They will check the date by your signature against your visa and will return to deport you."

His words gave her a new concern, but she couldn't let him see it. "Then I'll just renew my papers," she said.

Sammy shrugged.

An officer from the search force had been waiting nearby. The chief-inspector turned to him, and the officer snapped a palm-up salute. The two policemen moved a distance away and talked.

Leslie looked at Sammy. "Don't look so sad," she said. "This is what I want. Tell Mary that at last I've found a place where I can be happy. And tell her that I finally have students who want to learn."

The officer and the chief-inspector finished their conversation, and the officer saluted and returned to his troops. The chief-inspector ordered Sammy to the helicopter.

The machine's engine squealed to life, sending villagers back to their hiding places.

Leslie stepped back and looked at the chaos the police had wrought. Piles of belongings lay in front of the dwellings. Some of the structures had holes knocked in their sides, but apparently no people were hurt.

The two flying machines rose into the air simultaneously, a display of military precision for people who probably didn't appreciate the effort.

Leslie grabbed Jeiso's arm for support. She had extended her bravado to its limit, and her legs suddenly felt weak.

The helicopters whopped over the horizon, and Leslie leaned against the old man. He smiled a toothy grin and fumbled under his robes for the rhino-horn handle of his knife.

She stood in the courtyard until she could hear no more whopping sounds. Then she went to her dwelling and tried to restore order to the shambles. Several of her most recent class notes were missing but nothing else.

The only thing of Firingin's in the hut was the silk cloak he'd worn at their wedding. It was still hanging there.

None of the children from her school were anywhere in sight. They'd probably run to their homes as soon as the helicopters landed.

Firingin's eyes were wild when he entered the dwelling. He looked around in the dimness.

Leslie sat on the blankets, still quaking from her ordeal.

When Firingin saw her, he smiled. "You are all right?" he said. She nodded.

"I saw the flying machines."

"The police were here. They wanted me to go back, but I told them no."

"And they are gone now forever?"

"They will return. We must leave this village."

He looked long at her, and she saw his eyes grow moist.

"It is no longer safe," she said.

She felt tears flowing. "Maybe we should just give up. We can't have this life, can we?"

He had crawled to the doorway and was looking at the sky. He looked back at her. "I will talk to Jeiso," he said. "My real father lives in a village to the North. We will go there for our life."

She hugged him, shivering against his side.

"I will take the young she-camel," he said. "She will start my herd in the new village. You can open another school. And soon, our baby will be born."

She pressed her cheek to his shoulder. He seemed confident, but she knew him. He was as fearful as she.

She patted his arm and started packing.